"I don't intimida[te]"

She refused to be scared off by his remarks about how difficult the job was. She had the stamina; she had the training.

"I knew that long before you walked in the door." He looked steadily at her, his eyes conveying an unforeseen regard. But there was something else in those eyes, a masculine warning, something...predatory.

A wayward thrill spread across her breasts, up her neck. She'd fantasized such a moment for so long and thought it all so unlikely. Her pulse skipped as she looked into his eyes, the blue of flame. Sometimes fighting fire with fire was more dangerous than playing with it.

"Are you flirting with me, Jack?" she asked boldly.

"If I were..." he began, then paused. "Maybe I should say, if I am flirting with you, Becky, I'd be disappointed if you fell for it."

She straightened. "So would I."

"Then we understand each other?"

"Perfectly." She thought she pulled that off nicely, that he couldn't detect the hope that simmered in her.

He looked away a moment, then crossed his arms over his chest. "Why is it that I'm not convinced?"

Dear Reader,

In the Colorado mountains, snow comes in on a gust of wind, reaching blizzard conditions in a matter of minutes. Here, the Rampart Mountain Rescue Team is never lonely. But this year there's even more activity than usual for the team, as not only Mother Nature but mystery is swirling in their midst.

Get snowbound with the ROCKY MOUNTAIN RESCUE trilogy by three of your favorite Intrigue authors. For thrills, chills and adventure, ROCKY MOUNTAIN RESCUE is the place to be. Next month, look for #459 *Follow Me Home* by Leona Karr.

We hope you enjoy all the books in the ROCKY MOUNTAIN RESCUE trilogy, where an icy blizzard rages...and heated passions burn!

Regards,

Debra Matteucci
Senior Editor & Editorial Coordinator

Watch Over Me
Carly Bishop

Harlequin Books

TORONTO • NEW YORK • LONDON
AMSTERDAM • PARIS • SYDNEY • HAMBURG
STOCKHOLM • ATHENS • TOKYO • MILAN
MADRID • WARSAW • BUDAPEST • AUCKLAND

ISBN 0-373-22454-0

WATCH OVER ME

CAST OF CHARACTERS

Becky Difalco—Called upon to pay for the sins of her father, all Becky ever wanted was someone to watch over her, and to watch over in return.

Jack Slade—A preacher's son, ex-FBI hostage negotiator and extreme-skiing chopper pilot, Jack could talk his way out of any scrape or blessing—save one...

Michael Watkins—The infamous terrorist, twenty-five years on the Most Wanted list, thought Becky would make a fine martyr for his cause...

Joe Aguilar—Becky's boss wanted her assurance that she would follow protocol.

Gunnar Schmit—The man the locals called the "village idiot," Gunnar was loyal to a fault.

Louis Difalco—Becky's father should have gone down in the annals for the capture of "The Bushwhacker."

Maeve Hennessey—Her tombstone sent a powerful message.

Zeb Tucker—His radio etiquette finally slipped on the desperate news of a Denver catastrophy.

Sam Rosenberg—Becky's FBI backup beat her to the scene.

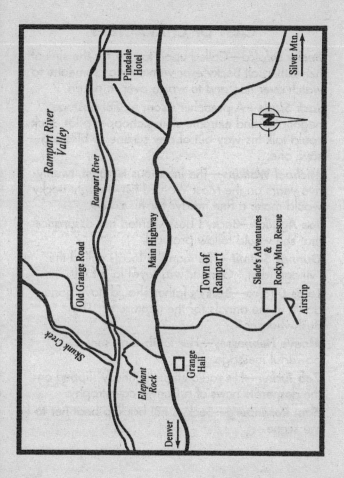

Prologue

On the first Tuesday in February, Michael Watkins began his simple morning ablutions well before dawn. He never slept until the sun came up in any case, but this day signaled the beginning of the end.

Only a few more days would pass before the murdering Feeb's daughter began to pay the final installment on the sins of her father.

A curious buzz of excitement, restlessness, quivered along the paths of his nerves. Purpose had revitalized him, placed him on this path. A bleak, withered shell resided in his chest where a beating heart would otherwise be found. Redemption wasn't possible, but justice, he believed, would out.

By the light of a kerosene lantern he peered into a mirror. The mirror had been cracked long before he found the thing and stuck it above the water pump in the lean-to-size cabin he'd outfitted to his purposes over the years. Staring into his dull brown eyes, he examined his face for signs of humanity remaining.

There were none.

He took out his silver shaving mug and brush, savoring for a few moments the scent of the cake of soap and the tension of the badger hairs in the brush, then lathered himself up and turned the straight-edge razor to a clean shave.

The soap was his only personal extravagance. The rich, exquisite scent, frothing into an uncommonly smooth and sublime lather, was all he needed to remind him—day in and day out, month after month, year after freaking year—what he was about. Why he was, after all, the Bushwhacker.

The Unabomber had nothing on Michael Watkins, nor had the cretins who had blown away half the Federal Building in Oklahoma City. He had extorted millions of dollars over the years, and every red cent of it he had returned, in one philanthropic way or another, to America's poor and downtrodden. Much like Robin Hood, Watkins had always believed, had his thieving predecessor access to modern-day explosives and the electronic transfer of currency.

Charity on such a scale no longer interested him. The poor were weak, the downtrodden morons, the oppressed were fools. No amount of money could save them. He believed now, after years of study, that if all the wealth in the world were equally distributed, it would inevitably find its way to the hands of the previously rich.

He no longer cared. He had no vision. His agenda had collapsed on itself until only revenge mattered.

Some clever federal agents believed Watkins had escaped to a banana republic from which he could never be extradited. Instead, he had simply gone nowhere but back to the mountains from whence he came.

Some of them, less clever, thought he'd grown old and tired. Or worse, lazy.

Some thought him dead. These were the most nearly accurate. Michael Watkins had been in a living hell for so many years, he could barely remember a time when it had been otherwise, or the years when he believed the score had been settled with the Feeb.

It wasn't.

Before he was done, he would have his reckoning.

Her name, carelessly uttered in an altogether different context, had triggered his imagination as much as his spite. The daughter must pay, he thought. The little girl grown up. The brave, stricken little dark-eyed waif of a child. The little girl who first captured the imagination of the country when her photo appeared on the cover of *Time* magazine, much like the baby in the fireman's arms twenty-five years later.

He doused his head and rinsed off the streaks of lather, suffering the frigid water straight from the rusty old pump. He must hurry. He dressed in long underwear, the least ragged of his two pairs of jeans, a heavy, nondescript pullover sweater and an army green, thirty-year-old goose-down jacket. He examined the three-corner tear where the snowy white goose down had been poking through for weeks.

He knew she was in Rampart. He'd stood and watched her, behind her back, searching, searching the films. Would she notice the three-corner tear, the spilling-out goose down, so that when she saw it again she would know for a certainty her turn had come to deal with the Bushwhacker?

Or should he have waved a flag under her nose? Maybe looked into the accommodating camera and given her a good long gander at his unpleasant, gap-toothed smile.

No. Difalco's daughter would prove a worthy opponent. The subtleties of his final act of revenge would be not be lost on her.

He took a chunk of jerky, tore off a piece with his teeth and stuffed the rest into his pocket, then took one last look around. Didn't take long, wasn't much to see. An old iron cot. A table, its rickety legs reinforced to bear the weight of his computer, on which he had launched his plan. He might have installed electrical lights, except for the fact that his computer and satellite dish consumed every watt of energy produced by the outdoor gas generator.

But after he left here today, four days prior to the twenty-fifth anniversary of The Outrage, capital *T*, capital *O*, his plan would take on a life all its own.

His ordinary brown eyes lingered on the solitary photo of Maeve. He could no longer bring to mind the scent of her skin, the texture of her shining auburn hair, the quality of her voice, the sound of her laughter, the profound sense of redemption he knew only in her arms.

On the other hand, he could picture Difalco's striking daughter in his mind's eye with ease. She had the wraith-pale complexion of the English in combination with Mediterranean dark hair, shapely eyebrows, a straight, barely freckled patrician nose and eyes so dark it was impossible to tell where her pupils left off and the irises began. Her mouth was overlarge, but the smile, when she smiled, made the sacrifice of perfection a blessing.

Her smile had become his target. He would wipe the joy from her lovely face forever, so that anyone who had ever loved her would be as hard-pressed as he to remember...

Enough, he thought savagely.

Enough.

What mattered was that Difalco's daughter had proven a quick study. An agent of the Colorado Bureau of Investigation white-collar crimes, of which extortion was one, she'd picked up on his subtle enticements. She'd caught the faint echoes of the Bushwhacker turning up here and there in bank transactions she monitored in her job.

She had ignored him for a while, refusing to rise to the bait, to hold herself accountable for what he might do. She had gone into law enforcement just like her father, but not, apparently, because she felt compelled to take up where he had failed.

Watkins had given her an opportunity to respond, to indicate via e-mail—many times removed so she could not trace the destination—that she would act to stop him from taking up his terrorist career again.

He admired her restraint. He respected her for refusing to live her life as a victim. But he had to have her, had to find a way to engage her, and so he'd locked up her personal computer with the photographic image of that baby in the fireman's arms.

He knew the deep wound in her well enough, and he knew she would not ignore him any longer.

She was very close now, but only at his invitation.

Did she sense the yawning death trap waiting for her?

He picked up his instrument of doom, a little plastic container, no bigger than a bathroom stickup—which was what it had been in another incarnation—and departed his falling-down cabin. He strapped on his cross-country skis and started down the snow-covered mountain.

He skied to the town of Rampart, where he left his boards against the side of the general store and caught the bus to Denver.

Five hours later, he walked the fifteen or twenty blocks to the U.S. Mint, his target. The symbol of everything wrong in this wildly extravagant country, the mint honored his history of extortion. No one would miss the irony. There he planted the sweet-smelling, death-dealing, satellite-triggered stickup in the men's john behind the toilet, bold as you please.

No flunky in the mint, no Treasury denizen, *no one* had detected anything amiss about his person, despite the high-tech security measures. He could feel little but disdain at the level of incompetence.

He boarded the bus to Rampart, satisfied that, unless his conditions were met, the Denver Mint and all the fair folk within ten city blocks were as good as ashes returning to ashes.

The biblical promise pleased him, where an eye for an eye had never sufficed. The Feeb's ill-fated daughter would return to ashes, as well.

Rebecca Difalco was, in his less than humble opinion, a born martyr.

Chapter One

It was only in her increasingly frequent nightmares that Becky Difalco ever truly remembered why. She had never expected to find herself tracking down the most reviled man on the nation's most wanted list. She'd been too young at five years old to consciously remember.

Traumatized, they'd all said. Unable, ever again, to believe in a benevolent world.

She refused to live like that, allowing people to treat her as if she would never have a thought or emotion or make a decision untainted by her terrifying childhood memories. At least she had until last night, when her personal computer had locked up on the nightmare image of another child. Another victim of a bombing, this one a baby.

Outside the small, dusty room where she had been sitting all day, snow had begun to fall in the mountain town of Rampart. The weather forecasters from Denver were predicting a significant threat of a high-country blizzard as of ten o'clock last night.

The warning made her nervous. The weather in the mountains could change inside ten minutes. As often as not, blizzards in the mountains failed to materialize as predicted or came roaring in with no notice at all.

She didn't have the luxury of believing she had one moment to waste. She had to put every second to use in the cramped storeroom the Rampart General Store used to double as an employee lunchroom. She turned on the video cam and focused again on the grainy, flickering images of video recordings from the security camera mounted over the ATM in the corner of the store. She'd been watching the same people come and go on the tapes for weeks on end—in the space of the last several hours.

Most security videos these days ran on a constant loop, taping over the previous twenty-four hours. This one, for some unknown reason, did not. The tapes were kept, changed, stored and used again in an eight-week cycle.

A lucky break? She didn't believe in luck.

Her search of these videotapes resembled nothing so much as a search for the proverbial needle in a haystack. She knew it well enough. But threads ran through banking transactions that were her responsibility to monitor, and the threads had come together in a pattern she had recognized as a private invitation to deal with Watkins. Threads specific enough to have brought her to this ATM and yet too insubstantial—far and away too trifling—to convince the powers that be, her superiors, that the Bushwhacker was back in business.

She had first spotted variations on the terrorist theme in banking transactions he had used in the past to carry out the extortion of entire cities.

Michael Watkins, a.k.a. the Bushwhacker, had blown up a full commuter train in Phoenix eleven years ago when the city refused to pay his ten-million-dollar demand.

He'd contaminated the city water supply in Beaverton, Oregon, unleashing a plague worthy of a Stephen King novel on the city.

He'd taken out the road to the Cheyenne Mountain installation where the U.S. Defense Command had charge of the nation's defense against nuclear attack—just to prove he could expose the jugular of the North American continent to any threat. And those were only the most extreme examples, the times when the authorities hadn't paid up.

This ATM was where the nebulous threads and patterns had led her.

Coincidence? No more than the fact that the security tapes were still available to her.

No. He had chosen his ATM carefully. He wanted her to have access to videotapes that were days, even weeks old. He wanted her to spot him.

She had refused the invitation, ignoring his bait for a long time, certain he was only toying with her. Mocking her for God alone knew what rhyme or reason.

The computer image of the child bombing victim had changed all that. She'd taken what leads she had and driven to Rampart from Denver in the middle of the night.

She put the video on pause again and rubbed her eyes. They felt gritty. Exhausted. As if, even if the Bushwhacker himself looked up and waved at her, she'd miss him. Trying to spot a man she had never seen who must have aged considerably and could have taken on any disguise was a nightmare all its own, especially since she believed he wanted her to find him.

"You doin' okay, missy? Doin' okay? Kin Gunnar getcha a soda? A soda?" An earnest, masculine voice interrupted her reverie.

Becky uncovered her eyes and glanced up to find Gunnar Schmit leaning on his push broom staring at her. She had heard some of the local middle schoolkids taunting Gunnar for being the village idiot.

Kids could be cruel, she thought, but they learned it all from grown-ups. She understood. He gave her the creeps the way he moved so silently, but his mental capacity had to be fairly impaired. He tended to repeat everything he heard and always referred to himself by his first name rather than the appropriate pronouns.

Still, she found Gunnar to be a sweet, wary man, a small-town, outsize Forrest Gump, intimidated by the gibes and insults and pitying looks pitched his way.

He stood at least six foot five, and he easily slung around his two hundred plus pounds of weight in cartons of canned goods and boxes of liquor.

She had also overheard him taking a call from Silver Mountain, the local ski area, where he operated the enormous Sno-Cats used to groom the ski slopes at night.

"Hello, Gunnar. My eyes are just on fire—"

"My eyes are just on fire, just on fire," he repeated in earnest. "Oh no, missy," he protested anxiously, peering at her. "They kin't go doin' that." He'd obviously taken her words literally.

"Not really, Gunnar. I'm just very tired of staring into this camera."

"Very tired," he commiserated.

"I would love a decaf soft drink if you have any cold ones." She was sticking hard to her resolve to get off caffeine, no matter how much she regretted it.

"Love a drink. Sure nuf." Gunnar leaned his broom against the wall inside the door and went to fetch her soda.

He departed and returned noiselessly with her soda and a grape soda for himself and sat at the head of the scarred old table on a rickety stool. She tried for a little while to make small talk with Gunnar, but it was like trying to converse with a mynah bird. She didn't have the patience.

"I'm going to get back to work now, Gunnar, if that's okay with you."

"Okay with you. Okay with you." He nodded, but made no move to leave.

She smiled idly, began the camera replay and focused tightly on the moving black-and-white— mostly shades of gray—images. If she hadn't come to know the regulars so well from her viewing hours, she might have passed right on by the man in the dark coat. Dark green? Navy?

He wore a ski hat pulled down over tangled, unkempt gray hair straggling to his coat collar. He moved differently than most people, angling his body and head in such a way as to minimize his exposure to the camera. Something of the man's bearded profile—perhaps the too-small nose or the overdeveloped forehead—made her mouth go dry in an instant.

She focused on the inadequate images. Her pulse thudded in her ears. She felt herself flushing. Like an animal catching the scent of fear, Gunnar tuned in to her reaction to the videotape and began to breathe hard.

"Something's wrong. Something's wrong," he parroted. "Kin Gunnar see? Gunnar see?"

She swallowed, nodded and rewound the tape. He might recognize the man in the video image. It would be a stroke of sheer luck if he knew where she could find the old man.

She held the camera so Gunnar could watch the

replay. His eyes narrowed as he watched, then he grinned. "That's old Mick, sure nuf, old Mick."

Mick. Short for Michael? Becky stared at Gunnar. The fondness in his tone made her uneasy. "Mick?"

"Yep. That's old Mick. See here. Had that tear in his coat too long. Too long, Gunnar told him. Better fix it 'efore all the stuffin's gone out."

Watching over Gunnar's shoulder, she saw the tiny three-cornered tear. It would take years for all the stuffing to come out, but that was the sort of detail Gunnar seemed to fixate on.

"Guess he don't like his picture took, his picture took, huh?" he said, grinning.

As simple as Gunnar might be, he understood the same body language she had picked up on. Old Mick *didn't* like having his picture taken. This man, if he was in fact the man she had been seeking, was protecting himself from the camera, from being recognized, after all these idle years hidden away in a small mountain town.

But no. He wanted her to spot him. This was Michael Watkins acting suspicious enough to insure she wouldn't overlook him.

"Hey." Gunnar must have sensed her doubt. He reared back on his stool, narrowing his eyes in suspicion at her. "You're...he's not a bad man, old Mick's not. What're you tryin' to do?"

Becky swallowed hard; threatened by Gunnar's intensity. Could he be persuaded that old Mick was a bad man? Would Michael Watkins's face on a most wanted poster do it? Or would Gunnar turn against her for bad-mouthing a loyal crony? "Old Mick a friend of yours, Gunnar?"

"A friend. Sure nuf. A friend of yours." The expression in Gunnar's already suspicious eyes hardened. "Thought you was lookin' for a bad man, very bad. A very bad man."

She couldn't lie. He'd noticed Mick's body language on camera, as well as her doubt at having let him see who caught her interest. Gunnar would sense her dissembling. "I am looking for a very bad man, Gunnar."

"Not him," Gunnar stated. "Not him, not Mick, sure nuf not Mick."

"Not him." She had to be careful. "But maybe Mick knows the man I am looking for," she went on. "He might be able to help me. Do you know any bad men in Rampart, Gunnar?"

His features twisted, more resentful than angry, she thought. "Some," he answered simply.

"Some?"

"At the Ram." The local night spot, Becky knew. "Just jerks, Jack Slade says."

Slade. The name arrested her attention, made her pulse skitter. It wasn't as if she didn't know Jack was in Rampart. She knew he'd taken to the high country when he'd left the FBI. She'd seen signs advertising his extreme-adventures enterprise at the edge of town.

She had a sort of abbreviated history with Jack

Slade. He'd asked her out years ago, when she'd been a rookie at CBI and he'd been the FBI's hotshot, go-to man in hostage situations from San Diego to Chicago.

She'd accepted, many times.

He was tall, at least shoulders above her, and powerfully built, dark-haired and keel-over-dead good-looking. No sane, sighted, unattached, normal female refused Jack. But when she understood how fast and hard she was falling in love, and how devastated she would be when Jack moved on, she'd broken it off.

Jack Slade always moved on. Which was why she had gone out of her way to avoid running into him in Rampart. Word had it that the last thing Jack wanted was a reminder from his past.

A peculiar curiosity flickered in Gunnar's features, then vanished. "Jerks," he repeated. "Old farts make Gunnar sick, sure nuf sick. Jack Slade alwus makes 'em back off and leave me 'lone, leave Gunnar be."

"Where is Jack now?"

She wanted to bite her tongue. His whereabouts had nothing to do with her. She should have closed off the subject of Jonah, a.k.a. Jack Camden Slade, but she could never let sleeping dogs lie. Never not know what there was to know.

It came, she was told, from some deep psychological need to anticipate and prepare for the next threat coming at her. When your house was leveled and you were only five and inside it, you got to be that way ever after.

"Where is Jack Slade now," Gunnar repeated, leaving off the rising inflection of a question. "Rampart Rescue. Used to be a cop but no one's supposed to know. Flying skiers in his chopper now. Always flying his chopper. Not at night, though. Not at the Ram."

The life-style Gunnar described rang true. Jack was ex-FBI, emphasis on ex. He would be of no help to her.

She had to get whatever information she could from Gunnar. His conception of a bad man apparently extended only to whoever treated him badly. Trying again, she gave him the benefit of the doubt. "I was thinking more in terms of crooks. Thieves. Murderers. Bad men like that."

"Bad men like that. How come? Are you a cop?"

"Yes. Sort of. I'm with the Colorado Bureau of Investigation."

Intent on his own point, for the first time he went on without repeating some part of what she had said. "You better be leavin' Mick alone. Nobody messes with Mick," Gunnar warned. "You leave him be. Mick don't mess with folks 'round here, 'n' nobody messes with him."

Her hands were shaking. She shut off the camera. "Listen to me very carefully, Gunnar. Please."

"Very carefully," he repeated dully, still giving her a mistrusting look.

She would have to be very careful herself. "I think my father and Mick might have known each other back in the seventies. I think Mick might be able to help me figure things out."

"Figger things out. Like what things?"

She touched Gunnar's sleeve. "Gunnar, people make fun of my dad, too, just like the jerks at the Ram sometimes hassle you. If I find Mick, maybe he can help me make them stop, like Jack Slade makes them back off jerking you around. I don't think Mick likes that, either."

"Jerking Gunnar 'round." He looked at her. "Mick don't like folks jerkin' folks like Gunnar 'round. Is y'r daddy slow, too?"

"No. But he drinks way too much."

Gunnar nodded nonstop, as if he understood, as if he were sympathetic and knew all about the ignominy her father endured. But really, there weren't many of his old colleagues left to jerk Louis Difalco's chain anymore. He did it to himself.

"Booze'll do that to a man," Gunnar said. "Booze 'n' a guilty conscience." The words came out singsong, together by rote, like ham and eggs.

Becky swallowed hard and gave a quick nod. No pretense was necessary when talking about her dad. He'd let Michael Watkins escape, and he would go to his grave with the guilt and the alcohol. "Will you help me, Gunnar? Will you tell me where I can find Mick, or where he lives?"

"Where Mick lives. Rabbit Foot Hill."

"Where is that? Can you tell me specifically, or point it out on a map?"

Gunnar considered for several long moments, then got up from the table to man his push broom again. "Nah," he finally allowed. "But if'n anybody starts messin' with your daddy, you just tell old Mick, and he'll put a stop to it, he will."

Becky clamped down hard on her frustration. Michael Watkins was the last man alive who would put a stop to the pain that had roared through Louis Difalco's head for going on twenty-five years. She would not have taken on the responsibility herself. She could not save her father, and she'd always known that.

But, for the memory of a lifeless child draped in the arms of a fireman, she would find a way to stop Michael Watkins.

She would simply have to take her search elsewhere.

Her best bet, knowing that Watkins lived close by, was to check out the utilities. He had to have a high-tech computer to pull off the ATM racket that had brought her here in the first place. He must have either electrical service or a gas-powered generator. Which in turn meant that, however self-sufficiently the Bushwhacker lived, he was not without at least that one tie to civilization.

With a little luck, she would find Michael Watkins very soon, even without Gunnar Schmit's help. But by then, she would need real assistance.

Watkins would not go gently.

Chapter Two

Slade guided his chopper, Lucy in the Sky Like Diamonds—he called her Lucy for short—through the craggy killer peaks of the Never Summer Range in northern Colorado. The extreme skiers he had ferried to the northern slope of the westernmost peak had come upon dangerously unstable snowpack.

The guide, an old Dane with more raw courage and common sense than any man alive, had radioed for an immediate evacuation. Willi Davidsen-Nielsen could hear an avalanche coming. Something in the air, he would say, as if that explained his foreknowledge. As if anything could.

Jack's trick now would be getting them out fast, without the roar of the chopper blades triggering the deadly avalanche.

Adrenaline ricocheted through his system like the words "Hallelujah, brother" in an old-time tent revival. This was the infamous edge where he lived, where the only lives ever lost were lost in the straight-up, honest risk of a man-versus-nature contest. He let rip with one hallelujah just for the hell of it, but he could barely hear himself over the whine of the engine and the roar of the chopper blades.

His old man would roll over in his sanctimonious grave to hear Jack's unbridled and ill-conceived blasphemy. Especially over the high he got from these thrills and chills, from flitting through the rarefied oxygen and the solid granite peaks of the Rockies in his chopper.

He didn't pull macho stunts with Lucy. His liability insurance for the kind of flying he did was higher than Mount McKinley. He couldn't afford missteps, so to speak, and so he had the best safety record in the United States or Canada, where extreme skiing was really big.

But honest challenge, to have lives depending on his skill, to take Lucy to the limits of her tolerances, this was almost as good as sex, which, he thought wryly, was a damned good thing.

This was living.

This was life on the top of the world. He didn't need any other kind of responsibility and he rejected the first syllable of a stray thought to the contrary.

But to make the whole proposition a little more interesting, a blizzard was coming faster than a...well, he wouldn't go there. His old man would roll over all over again. There wasn't a time Jack could remember when he hadn't had the deepest contempt for his father's tent-revival, holy-roller, holier-than-thou, call-me-saved antics.

Somehow the recrimination in his father's fire-and-brimstone voice had come to mind twice inside thirty seconds, and that scared the bejesus out of Jack.

He turned his attention to his coordinates and flight panel, then to the ground, then saw the skiers waving from below and to his left. He would not be able to set down. He had known that from Willi's distress call. Which meant a pretty hairy evacuation, hovering above ground close enough to the earth to get the skiers aboard without wrapping the blades around a tree or giving the fragile snowpack the first excuse to slide.

He gauged his descent, worked his collective pitch and the cyclic with finesse and extraordinary precision. Coming in low to the ground, he watched Willi for any danger signals and kept the chopper blades at an angle to minimize the possibility of triggering the avalanche.

Ducking into the prop wash, Willi opened the passenger door and began shoving the half-dozen skiers into the chopper. The weight of each man added to the mix, requiring subtle adjustments Jack fought to maintain.

The wind had whipped itself into a frenzy, spiraling madly up the narrow canyon. The snowpack heaved and then cracked so loudly the fissure exploded over the noise of the engine and the chopper blades.

In that instant, with Willi left to board, Lucy bucked and dipped violently in the sucking dynamics of the wind and the wake of the avalanche. Despite Jack's iron-willed control, she rose at least six feet off the ground. The slide began three hundred feet down, but the shelf it took ended where Willi was left standing.

Jack swore vilely. Not about to lose the old fart, he bellowed at Willi, urging him to make a jump for it.

A down draft jerked at Lucy's tail rotor, and Jack corrected for all he was worth. The instant the shelf of snow exploded from beneath Willi, the old Dane made one hail-Mary leap at the sled runners, and from the drag on the right side of the chopper Jack knew he'd made it.

Relief flooded his veins. Willi would let go, if he ever let go, when hell froze over. Ascending at nearly a thousand feet per minute, Jack took Lucy where he could set down and get the old Dane inside the chopper.

At the nearest clearing large enough to accommodate the chopper, he eased her groundward. The snow was so thick he couldn't see squat. Willi took a free-fall from what Jack estimated to be ten feet and then got up and hobbled along till the skiers could pull him through the door.

Jack expected a high five and a yelp or a triumphant yodel from Willi, but his face was ashen, the expression in his blue eyes stricken, and he couldn't utter so much as a whimper for trying to catch his breath.

"Get him the goddamned oxygen," Jack hollered, lifting off again. One of the skiers got his rattled wits together and snatched up the emergency oxygen mask. Another one twisted the canister spigot open, and the flow of oxygen began. Willi clamped the mask to his face and collapsed on the floor.

Jack turned Lucy toward Rampart and radioed for medical assistance, ETA thirty-one minutes. He took the chopper to twenty thousand feet, Lucy's service ceiling, to get above the blizzard that had come on so fast Jack had never seen its like.

He'd seen his share. Flown through enough in the unpredictable Rockies to have quite a healthy respect for Mother Nature's nasty little jokes. At fifteen minutes out, he radioed to the headquarters of Rampart Mountain Rescue operations, which were housed in his building.

Zeb came on the radio. "You better be hightailin' it back, Jack," the old man warned. "Over."

"What are the ground conditions?"

"The wind's howling down something fierce off the fourteeners, and it's a cold bitch, too. Snow's piling up at higher elevations. Gettin' word of folks off the road over Rabbit Ears Pass, 'n' out toward Hal's ranch some pregnant lady's stranded. Jill's in back now getting ready to head on out and see if she can help. Over.''

Scanning his instruments, trying to will vision through the whiteout conditions below Lucy's hull, Jack grimaced. Rampart Mountain's volunteer rescue team was among the finest anywhere, but chronically short-staffed. "How's the call-out board?"

"Ain't nobody ain't already out on some errand or another. Sheriff's dealing with a busload of kids. Bus broke down. Nothin' real serious yet, but all the same. Jill's had her hands full, I can tell you. Over."

Jill Gaylor had proved a fine coordinator for Slade's Adventures, acting as dispatcher for the rescue teams, as well. Her son, Randy, reminded Jack of his best friend in junior high. She hadn't been in Rampart long, though, and he worried about her going out. "Tell her to be careful, will you?"

"She's got a good head on her shoulders," Zeb reassured him. "Over."

"What about Doc Evanston? Where is he?"

"Skiing, last I heard, but he may be helping out with the kids. He ain't likely to be available. What y' got onboard? Over."

Zeb's by-the-book radio etiquette was wearing very thin. "Willi's gimped up and on oxygen. Severe frostbite, lung exposure, maybe a sprained or broken ankle."

Zeb let fly a blue streak. "Ornery old cuss. I'll kick his butt to Steamboat and back. You tell him I said so. Over."

"Yeah." Jack wished he had the heart. Willi *was* an ornery old cuss. Death had come calling at his door any number of times, but Willi finessed his way out of the final call every time. It would be on Jack's head if the old Dane suffered anything more than temporary damage. He signed off with Zeb.

Gutting it out, flying by the seat of his pants and accumulated experience of seven thousand, six hundred plus flight hours, Jack finally broke through the blizzard ceiling within fifteen miles of his target, the helipad he called home.

Though it had dumped a couple feet of snow in a two-hundred-degree arc surrounding the town, making the mountain passes and roads all but impassable, the blizzard had only just begun in Rampart. If he'd ever been more grateful for a break in the weather, he didn't know when. He'd lost his adrenaline high as soon as he'd looked into Willi's dauntless, haunted eyes.

The real problem was, no matter how many years had passed, no matter the good times or the adrenaline highs or how Jack ran, he could never quite forget the other haunted eyes. Thirty-one pairs in all, every member of the sixth-grade class of McCormick Middle School in the southeast Denver suburb of Highlands Creek.

GUNNAR LUMBERED out of the storeroom whistling a tune. After zipping the carrying case with the camera and identifying tape inside, Becky threw on her winter parka and picked up her purse. She waved goodbye to Gunnar and Irma, the clerk and cashier, then walked quickly through the biting wind to her motel room a couple of blocks down Main.

She eased her load onto the small blond Danish modern dresser, discarded her parka, then sat on the bed to make the necessary call. She punched in her personal calling card number and reached her boss on his private line within a few seconds.

She told Joseph Aguilar she was onto a perp in Routt County and needed immediate assistance.

"What the hell does that mean?" he demanded. It wasn't her position to be rounding up criminals. Especially on her own. "Who exactly are we talking about?"

Cut-to-the-chase Joe, she thought. How else had she thought this conversation would go? "Joe, please don't make this difficult for me. You know—"

"Becky." A thick sort of silence filled the space after his interruption. "It's Watkins you think you're onto, isn't it?"

"Yes. It's him. It's Michael Watkins. I'm certain of it, Joe."

"Where are you?" he demanded, although what she was meant to hear was the subtext. *Have you lost your mind?* "Are you on your pager?"

"Rampart. Yes, I've got my pager, and no, I haven't lost it. Joe, I have the most wanted felon in three decades and—"

"I don't care if you have the reincarnation of Genghis Khan dead to rights, Difalco," Aguilar snapped, cutting her off. "Do you *want* to wind up like your old man, or what?"

"Or what, sir," she snapped. She knew his temper was motivated more by her safety and well-being than anything, but the crack about her father was meaningless.

Yes, she was Louis Difalco's daughter. Yes, Watkins had handpicked her for the role of adversary. But the truth was, neither her father's bitter and oddly secretive recriminations nor the mess he had made of his life had anything at all to do with her.

And Aguilar had not had the benefit of seeing the death-dealing image Watkins had used to freeze her computer.

"You would have to assume that Watkins will prevail, that I have no chance of bringing him in, Joe, to believe I could ever end up like my father. That isn't going to happen, but even if it does, I am not my dad.

"I have to try to stop a madman before he strikes again, and I may fail. But if I do, it won't be because I didn't give it my best shot. And it won't mean that I am a worthless human being, either."

"Are you finished?" Aguilar demanded, his voice curving low in anger and sadness.

"No." She hated the sound of sadness on her behalf. Despised it with everything inside her. She donated most of her free time to various victims' assistance programs around Denver. She wasn't the only child ever to have lost her mother, but you would think, by the way people soft-pedaled around her, that she was.

"There's something inevitable about all of this, Joe," she went on. "I've been deliberately drawn here. Watkins apparently lives like a hermit at a place called Rabbit Foot Hill. I have to assume he knows I'm here. He's done everything but give me his GPS coordinates. And he will strike again, unless I stop him."

Aguilar swore softly. "Yeah, well, Global Position this, Difalco. You're out of your league. I'm telling you now. At best, if you're right, his capture is the jurisdiction of the FBI. I'm ordering you to stand down."

"That's a load of crap, Joe, and you know it! If we had the time to get a full-fledged squad in here, then fine."

"Becky, it's still nothing that can't wait forty-eight hours."

She removed a small silver loop earring, then transferred the phone receiver to take out the other one. "You're wrong, Joe. If I don't act on this, something terrible is going to happen. Can you live with that outcome, Joe? If dozens more people die because we didn't take him seriously and do whatever it took to stop him?"

The silence on the other end of the line spoke for his uneasiness. "Why doesn't any of this follow

Watkins's m.o., Becky? There hasn't even been an extortion attempt...unless there's something you haven't told me.''

She took a deep breath. Again, what she took for a direct threat, Joe might construe differently. In any case, she had no proof linking Watkins to any real threat.

She simply knew.

''There was something, Joe. There is. I would have told you about it, but I just got in the car and drove up to Rampart last night.'' She didn't have to describe the image of the bloodied child locking up her computer monitor to Joe. ''Maybe it can all be traced to him eventually. But by then it might be too late.''

Aguilar swore in his native Spanish. He knew the toll in human lives the Bushwhacker was capable of exacting. ''If it is Watkins,'' he insisted quietly, ''then the proper jurisdiction is still with the Feds, and they'll get him. I'll call the Colorado division and see if there isn't some way to get into Rampart. I'll put my ass on the line that far for you. I'll even go so far as to say you should stick around and wait for them.''

''I appreciate it, Joe. I mean that.''

''I mean what I say, too, Becky,'' he warned.

''I know you do.''

''You *wait*. You treat this as if you were an informant. You tell the FBI who you think you've identified and where he is, and you let them do their job. You can consider that a direct order, and if you don't like it, you can consider yourself consigned to the secretarial pool for the rest of your natural life. Are we clear on—"

"Yes," she interrupted, grateful for even this limited authorization. "Call the FBI. Tell them I need backup and I need it in the next twenty-four hours."

She replaced the receiver in the cradle, took up her purse and went searching for better answers than Gunnar had been willing or able to give her as to the whereabouts of Michael Watkins.

THOUGH JOE had promised to let her know as soon as he had a commitment from his FBI contacts, he hadn't called by the time the news came on television at ten o'clock that night. She'd gotten her break in pinpointing Watkins's lair.

She needed another one. Badly.

More anxious with each passing hour, she finally picked up the phone in her motel room and tried to call Joe at home.

The phone lines, it turned out, had been jammed or were down altogether. According to news reports, the blizzard threatening Rampart had socked in the rest of the northern Colorado Rockies. Local calls were apparently still going through, but she couldn't even get an operator on the line to put through an emergency call.

She turned off the lamp at her bedside and dozed for a while, but real sleep eluded her. Cut off from the outside world altogether, she had no way of knowing whether the Feds were coming at all.

Attempting to take Watkins in herself bordered on the foolhardy. She knew that. And somewhere around three in the morning she came around again to the possibility she knew Joe Aguilar worried about—that Watkins wanted only her. That as Louis Difalco's daughter, she was the Bushwhacker's final target.

He could well be lying in wait for her, intending no other harm.

If he was planning an ambush, he had every advantage and she had no chance of surviving so much as a scouting expedition anywhere near him. There was no assistance to be had. In Rampart, the closest the sheriff ever got to any kind of trouble was hunters taking game out of season.

She didn't believe it. Couldn't believe that even if she was Watkins's ultimate target, the last piece of his revenge, he would conceive a plan so utterly lacking in flair and vengeance as to take her out in an inglorious, anonymous ambush.

She turned on the bedside lamp and powered her laptop computer. She stuffed the pillows behind her back and checked the e-mail the computer had automatically downloaded. A couple of news group updates. A couple of friends checking in to say hello. Her cross-country ski club announcing the spring trip. Five messages from her colleagues at victims' assistance…

And then, a message from Aguilar. Subject—quarry.

Her heart thumped. She selected Aguilar's missive and chewed her lip for the few seconds it took to come onto the screen. "FBI SA Sam Rosenberg," it read, "already in Rampart on ski trip. Will meet, assess and assist in capture if possible at 0—"

But there it broke off without the final lines of transmission documentation. Becky swore softly. She could pinpoint the exact moment the long-distance phone lines had gone dead in Rampart. Eight thirty-eight twenty-four. The cost of knowing that was the crucial missing information in Aguilar's message to her.

When and where would Rosenberg meet with her to assess and assist in the capture of Michael Watkins, a.k.a. the Bushwhacker?

"Great." The irony of it made her crazy. Her favorite teacher had once assured Becky's fifth-grade class that with every dark cloud there came a silver lining. Becky had spouted her own version. *With every silver lining came a dark cloud.*

Which earned her a trip to the principal's office.

She'd adored Mrs. Beal anyway, and Mr. Zachman had only scolded her and required her to feed the fish in the aquarium in his office every school day for a month.

She'd never quite gotten the knack of playing Pollyanna.

Life wasn't always so tough. She knew that. She

had walked away from more black clouds than had ever rained on her parade. She wasn't a wet blanket, and her friends would have said Becky was only careful, not a dyed-in-the-wool pessimist.

But in her heart and in her experience, when it mattered, things were more likely to go wrong than to go right.

Now, miraculously, here in Rampart was the federal agent she needed, the perfect silver lining to an already black cloud, and she had no way of finding him.

A part of her wondered if she wouldn't be far better off ignoring Watkins, as she had early on. To force his hand. He wanted her attention. He wanted her to know what he was up to and how powerless she was to stop it. What if the only way to frustrate his plan, whatever that may be, was to refuse to play along at all?

It would work for a while. Hours, even days, perhaps. Enough time to get a fully manned operation together to execute his capture. The more she thought about it, the more sense it made. Watkins had gone to great lengths to command her attention.

She exited her e-mail and went to the files she had put together to search for something she had missed. Anything. The smallest hint of Watkins's larger intentions. She had been through it all a hundred times, and this attempt wasn't proving much different.

This is futile, Becky. The thought wouldn't be ignored. She should try to sleep, she knew, to get some rest. But she wouldn't sleep, so what was the point?

She started, at the beginning, choosing the chronological file of the Bushwhacker's terrorist career. She'd carefully constructed the data-bank format weeks before when she needed some way to make sense of what she was finding in the eleventh-district banking records.

She began to fiddle with the various categories in the data bank of the Bushwhacker's exploits. She tried ordering the events by location, then by the federal agents involved, then by the witnesses, then by the dates.

If she hadn't been bleary-eyed, seeing double or believing she must be seeing double, she would have missed it. But the February 5 on the date-and-time function at the bottom of her screen matched the February 5 at the bottom of the chronology page. And when she blinked and blinked again, the two remained separate and distinct.

February 5 was the twenty-fifth anniversary of the day the Bushwhacker had escaped her father's dragnet.

She shivered violently to shake off the sudden chill. This was it, then, proof of what she had sensed must be true. That he was ready to act. That the invitation to play his depraved games had been carefully timed to coincide with his historic escape.

Michael Watkins wanted to make another statement.

The Bushwhacker craved notice the way a dying man craves one more hour.

Maybe what he wanted most was for her—the all-important daughter—to be here, to witness firsthand exactly how he intended to prevail.

The street lamps and neon signs reflected off the snow and shone through the inadequate motel room curtains. With only the most irrational hope that she would connect with the FBI agent in Rampart, she shut down her computer and lay sleepless in her bed.

She thought again of Jack and the seventeen hours leading up to his monster fall from grace. No one had faulted Jack but himself. Not the heartbroken families, not his peers, not the community, not even the press—who would have second-guessed the Second Coming.

If anyone on earth could have prevented the madman's heinous shooting spree in that middle-school classroom, it was Jack Slade.

He'd left the FBI and transformed himself into one king-of-the-mountain, never-look-back, never-say-die, take-no-prisoners party animal. She understood, but in her mind, good people couldn't opt out. You pulled up your socks and you swallowed your load of guilt and you went on to save other lives.

She was in this one alone.

At the first light of dawn, she climbed out of bed and got on the phone. Local calls were still going through. She went through meager directory listings of every bed-and-breakfast and hotel in Routt County, checking for a guest registered under the name of Sam Rosenberg.

There were none, which meant he must be staying with friends or at a friend's condo—either way, impossible to find.

She gave up the search, then showered and dressed to her teeth against the biting wind and flurries of snow. She checked her firearm, tucked it inside her boot and left her motel room.

Her boots crunched through the snow in the direction of the diner the truckers and all the early-morning businesspeople frequented. The truck stop, reminiscent of something out of a fifties movie, was packed with men whose rigs were stranded in Rampart.

A figure of Gunnar Schmit's size and build sat at the far end of the counter, head down, bent over a stack of pancakes. She moved carefully into a position where she could determine if he was Gunnar.

The man turned suddenly and fixed his eyes on her. Her heart slammed against the wall of her chest. The last person she wanted to encounter was the gentle giant whose loyalty to Michael Watkins could still interfere with what she had to do. She turned away as if she had been searching for a place to sit. The man at the counter was not Gunnar.

In the entire diner the only person she recognized was the older of the two waitresses. Becky found one empty stool at the far right end of the breakfast counter, ate what carbohydrates and protein she could force down, then asked the teenage girl pouring her decaf for the phone number of the truck stop.

She took down the number on a napkin. "Are the local phone lines still working?"

"Far as I know. But you're already here," the girl pointed out helpfully.

"Thanks. I remember now."

The teenager rolled her eyes.

She walked to the entrance alcove of the diner where she could watch everyone present without being seen herself, pulled out her cell phone and punched in the diner number. The older waitress picked up the phone at the entrance to the kitchen.

Becky made her request. "I've been separated by the storm from my friend. Would you mind asking if he's in your diner?"

"Sure," the woman muttered. "I've got all day. Where are ya?"

"The...uh, the gas station at the opposite end of town," Becky lied. The most direct thing to do would have been to stand in the middle of the diner and ask if Rosenberg was there. To be on the safe side, she didn't want anyone to know where she was or what she was doing.

Using the cell phone gave her one last crack at finding Rosenberg without drawing attention to herself.

"What's the name?" the waitress demanded.

"Rosenberg." Becky spelled it, then repeated the name. "I'm looking for Sam Rosenberg."

The woman turned and bellowed, "Anybody here by the name of Rosenberg?" The waitress looked around impatiently. No one stood or answered her.

Jamming the back of her hand against her lips to stifle a frustrated sigh, Becky hung up, folded the cell phone and put it away.

She bundled up again and left the diner. It took her car engine a couple of tries to catch and turn over. She gave it a few minutes more to warm up, then backed up and took the highway that cut through the middle of Rampart, heading to the narrow excuse for a side road one turn to the west beyond the Old Grange Road. Rabbit Foot Hill wasn't on any map, just a designation the locals used.

She'd planned her approach after getting Aguilar's halfhearted blessing yesterday afternoon. Just before five, when it was already dark and the freezing cold air stung her nose, she'd finally gotten her break.

She found the man who delivered propane to old Mick's place.

The name on the invoices was Mick Hennessy. She'd claimed to be looking for an old friend of her father's, a man named Mick whose last name she couldn't remember. The guy at the scarred wooden counter chuckled and allowed as how there wasn't any other Mick in all of Routt County but this Hennessy fellow—whom a woman alone would be well advised to skip looking up.

"The guy's a hermit. Can't say as I've ever actually seen him. Nuttier than a fruitcake, if you ask me. Has this satellite setup you would *not* believe, but he don't even have an indoor crapper. Got himself the damnedest outhouse."

"You're kidding."

"No, I'm not, either. Fact is, Mick's not what you'd call the welcoming kind. Heard tales he totes a twelve-gauge shotgun by way of greeting unexpected guests."

"All the same," she mused. "It would help me out a lot if you could point me in the right direction."

"You seriously gonna head on up there anyways?"

"Not till morning," she replied. "I'll just see how it goes. My dad is dying. It would mean a lot to him to get word of Mick."

The guy shrugged, wiggling his mustache in a matching gesture. "It's your neck."

He'd shown her on the map exactly where he made deliveries to Mick Hennessy's tumbledown cabin, and the route he took to Rabbit Foot Hill.

"Road's rutted pretty bad. You'll have a devil of a time spotting it, so look for an old break in the snowbank. S'pose you drive one of them foreign tin cans."

She smiled. "I suppose I do. Is there any other way up there?"

"There is, but not in a vehicle. It's a considerable hike over the top. I can tell you right now, young lady," he warned, glaring at her boots, "those fancy-assed boots weren't made for that trek. However the dickens you get there, you watch out. Myself? Wouldn't wanna tangle with no sawed-off twelve-gauge greetin'."

The boots weren't a problem. In her trunk she carried all her climbing and rescue equipment, including a well-worn pair of boots and liners for hiking through snow. But she didn't intend to get close enough for Watkins to blast her to bits.

She had planned on getting the lay of the land, the obstacles to be overcome. She had needed a plan in time to brief Rosenberg.

But as she plowed through snow piling at nearly an inch per hour, she knew all bets were off. She had missed Aguilar. The cavalry wasn't coming. All she could do was go by her instincts, hoping she would have at least the advantage of taking Watkins by surprise.

She found the road leading up the mountain and slogged through sleet and snowdrifts, driving as far as her front-wheel-drive sedan could manage. Pulling over to the side of the road until the car tilted at a near thirty-degree angle, she tried to imagine what it would be like, what she would do when she got to Watkins's cabin.

Her heart thumped slowly. A cowardly part of her wanted desperately to turn back or find another way or look up Jack Slade and make him understand what was at stake. Beg him to back her up.

Anything, in short, to avoid taking on Watkins by herself.

The man had masterminded mass murder. Did she seriously suppose she could take him by surprise? Take him at all?

But even if she could find Slade, even if she could convince him to come out of his self-indulgent retirement to help her stop Michael Watkins before it was too late, would it be too late already?

Breathing out, determined to override her fears and do what was in front of her to do, she switched off the car and got out. There would be no more dithering, waiting for nonexistent help.

She knew exactly what she must do. She'd known since thirty seconds after she learned Watkins's place had no indoor plumbing.

He would have to leave his cabin to use the outhouse. Sooner or later he would have to come outside, and then she would have her chance. She would catch him then, without his sawed-off shotgun, and make her arrest. But if he made a run for it, if it came to that, she would shoot to drop him, whatever it took.

Her plan was only marginally less practical with one shooter rather than two. She couldn't imagine the prospect of being the one to lie in ambush, but she had no choice. Watkins was directly responsible for the deaths of one hundred and ninety-seven innocent men, women and children.

She had to stop him before he stripped even one more child of its family, or a family of its children.

The snow was coming steadily down, but curiously, there was no wind. Closed in by the towering pine forest, she knew she could approach Watkins's cabin by hiking straight up the mountainside, no more than half a mile, maybe three-quarters.

The road on the map twisted and turned, but she could cut the distance in half this way, and keep herself concealed, as well.

She checked her firearm one more time, placed it in the deep outer pocket of her parka and stashed a small pair of binoculars in her other pocket, then began her ascent.

The snow was hip deep in places, having piled up for months, and the vertical pitch was nearly impossible to negotiate. She battled her way up the rocky, snow-packed incline for nearly two hours before she heard the distant intrusion of an aircraft engine impinging on the silence of the wilderness.

Breathing hard from the subzero cold and from exertion, she looked up, trying to get a sense of the noise, and while she wasn't paying attention to her footing, caught her boot on some rock buried beneath the snow and went down hard. A sharp stabbing pain shot up from her knee the moment she recognized the sound as the heavy thwack of chopper blades.

A helicopter? In this weather? Here, so near Watkins's lair?

Alarms went off inside her head. Still not within sight of the cabin, she scrambled up the mountain, the pain in her knee all but obliterated by the adrenaline rush to reach her quarry. She clung to naked aspen saplings, pulling, fighting for purchase every halting step of the way, conscious at each and every moment of the mounting shrill whine of a helicopter engine.

She heard the engine wind down, the distant shouts, the continual whopping of the helicopter blades, and then, reaching a plateau, she saw Watkins's propane tank and a satellite dish, broken-down stairs and a door banging fiercely in the wake of the AirLife rescue chopper lifting off.

No more than thirty seconds later, the propane tank exploded, making a fiery crater of the mountain cabin from which she assumed Michael Watkins had just escaped.

Chapter Three

At ten in the morning, with visibility reduced on the ground to about a car length, Jack drove to Willi's place. The Dane lived on a property Jack owned off the Old Grange Road, and once the blizzard got a stranglehold in the valley, Willi would be as shut in as an old maid. Jack had no trouble in his all-terrain vehicle getting to Willi's cabin, hauling in enough firewood to last a week or ten days and dropping off a few groceries.

Unfortunately, leaving before the craggy old fart could make some smart-ass comment didn't happen. Frostbite or no, his ankle seriously sprained, sporting tubes up his nose for continued oxygen therapy, Willi got off several amused looks and didn't stop there.

"Got a real talent there for nest making, Slade." Although Willi's English was idiom-perfect, his Scandinavian accent went invariably thicker with his taunts. "I'm just wondering if your eyesight's all it's cracked up to be."

Jack scoffed. Nest making wasn't in his future, and his eyesight was fine. Willi knew that. He was just taking another irritating stab at getting Jack's goat. He told Willi quite amiably to go to hell.

"Ha!"

"Ha, yourself." Tossing a couple of pots and pans and dishes and some silverware on the table so that getting around on his gimped-up ankle to feed himself wouldn't do the old man in, Jack glared amicably at Willi. "Got no time for a woman. Women, yes. One?" He shook his head.

"Only the good die young," Willi teased. "I know you think elsewise, but take my word for it. You won't be so lucky, so you might as well give up your dreams of going out in a blaze of glory and settle yourself down with a God-fearing woman. One that's not too hard on the eyes. There's Jill—"

"Oh, great." Jack gave a half-assed grin. Jill Gaylor was real easy on the eyes, but she wasn't his type. Besides, her son, Randy, needed the kind of stable role model Jack refused to be. "Wouldn't that be a hoot. Jack and Jill. Jack breaks his head and Jill tumbles to a broken heart and the poor innocent kid—"

"You're an arrogant cuss, you know that?"

"That's what I've been trying to tell you."

"Nothing I didn't already know." Willi jerked on his crutch, pointing at the door. "Case you hadn't noticed, there's a blizzard on out there. Might be a few folks who really need your help." His tone suggested that he sure didn't.

Jack shrugged into his coat and gave Willi an amiable but nonetheless rude gesture, muttering about ingrates. It made no sense at all, but he loved the coot. "Take care of yourself, Nielsen. I need your scrawny carcass on the job."

Willi returned an equally crude gesture. And on his way out the door, Jack thought he heard the old man muttering that Jack Slade didn't have a fig of a notion what he needed.

Bounding off the wooden porch, he laughed, even though the comment stung. He got in his solid black Explorer and took off in the direction of town. He reached the intersection with the highway, turned left. On the verge of figuring out why he gave a tinker's damn for Willi's opinion, he switched off the radio and heard the unlikely distant sound of chopper blades.

He pulled over, cut the engine and stepped out, listening hard. No point in looking. Visibility was about a hundred feet, but he wasn't mistaken. No one in his right mind would be flying in this, but the sounds he heard were undeniably chopper noise. A few seconds later came a muted thundering noise, like the blasting caps the avalanche control teams used. He frowned. In the ordinary course of things, Jack was consulted and advised of avalanche control measures.

He got into his vehicle and radioed Rampart

Mountain Rescue. "Rampart, this is Slade. Anyone copy?" A few seconds later, he repeated his message.

Zeb finally came on. "I copy, Jack. Jill's not in yet, and Randy's grabbing some shut-eye. Where are you?"

"Five minutes down the road. Did you hear anything about any blasting going on?"

"Not a word. Why? Over."

"What about a medevac chopper launch?"

"Here? In this weather? No way. Over."

"Zeb, I just heard one."

"You what? You heard one? How do you know it was medevac? Over."

"Just a guess. There isn't any other sane reason for being up." He steered around a snowbound subcompact, looking for stranded people. Seeing no one in or outside the car, he drove on. "Do me a favor, will you, Zeb? Try to find out what the situation is on the blasting and the chopper." Most flight-for-life choppers could only handle one critical patient at a time. If others were stranded and injured, he needed to know.

"We're down to radio communication, but I'll give it a shot. Over."

"Appreciate it. I'll be there shortly." He started to hang the mike on its hook, then thought, *What the hell.* Just to make Zeb's day, he depressed the transmit button and signed off all legal-like. "Slade, over and out."

BECKY CLAPPED her gloved hands over her ears.

The blast reverberated around her. Ducking under an immense Scotch pine, she watched flaming cinders landing in the snow a few feet from where she stood. Under the blizzard conditions and the months-old snowpack, the hot ashes wouldn't burn long enough to set the surrounding forest on fire. Still, the smell of them turned her stomach. Her ears ached with a ringing, and the force of the blast seemed to collapse her lungs.

Was this how she was supposed to have died?

She gave herself a mental shake and discarded the thought. There was no way Watkins would leave her demise to chance.

Maybe he'd seen her coming, despite her care. She couldn't see beyond the trees, but there could be a vantage point where he watched her drive in. There was no other explanation for the timing of his escape.

And the destruction of every piece of evidence that might ever be used against him. The Unabomber should have been so thorough.

Michael Watkins was no one's fool and every citizen's worst nightmare.

Shaking hard, caught in some never land between the paralyzing cold and her primitive flight-or-fight emotions, she crawled from under the tree and began scrambling the way she had come up.

Sliding on her backside down the more treacherous inclines, she tried to breathe through her nose to warm the bitter cold air before it hit her lungs. The altitude created enough of an obstacle. The extreme cold made the challenge a desperate one.

She rested to catch her breath at a boulder she thought must be nearly in sight of her car. She had made it almost down when her foot slid out from beneath her and she fell hard on her back, jolting her whole body, banging the back of her head on the frozen snowpack.

Pain shot through her shoulder and torso. Tears sprang to her eyes. She wanted to cry in anger and frustration, but the fall had knocked the wind out of her. Sitting up gingerly, she swiped at her tears, but it did little good, because what really mattered was that she had failed to stop the Bushwhacker.

Failed completely.

And it occurred to her finally that this must be what Watkins wanted. To escape from her at the last possible second, leaving her absolutely powerless to stop whatever carnage he had in mind.

A replay. A father-daughter tandem play, separated in time but in no other way. Michael Watkins's way of telling her, *Put this in your pipe, Becky Difalco, and smoke it.*

She might not be able to stop the tears, but she would never concede the deadly game. She had never intended this outcome. Never intended to make her life a campaign against Michael Watkins. Never wanted anything more than to do her job and do what she could for the victims of crimes.

But now, if there was one snowball's chance in hell of stopping him, this time or the next, she would find it.

She stuffed the pain, got to her car and mentally ran through what it would take for her to turn and drive down the mountain without getting her car stuck in a drift. She divided her attention between the perilous drive and her next move.

She had no choice but to take her story to Slade. The FBI had to be warned, and if anyone in these remote, socked-in mountains or the tiny little burg of Rampart would know how to do that, it would be Jack.

She followed the ice-encrusted signs to Slade's Adventures and pulled to a stop beside a jet-black, four-wheel-drive Explorer. She got out and stood a moment, steeling herself to deal with Jack, praying he was here and not out on some rescue.

Impatient with herself, she slammed the car door shut and walked into the low-slung building. The place seemed deserted, but she followed the sound of low, urgent male voices to the door with Slade's name on it.

One man, older, a little grizzled and tearing his hair out, manned a radio. Beside him, Jack Slade stood examining an intricate map on the far wall. Both men had their backs to her.

"What do you mean, the place went up?" the old man shouted, trying to compensate for the crackling interference. "This happened after you got the officer down call?"

The phone rang incessantly, giving the place an aura of pandemonium with no one there to deal with it. Each time, a feminine voice answered via the machine with the message, "You've reached Rampart Mountain Rescue. All available rescue personnel are out. Please leave a message, and we'll get to you as soon as possible. If this is a life-threatening situation, hang on the line and someone will pick up."

Becky put down her bag, shrugged out of her parka and hung it on a scarred old wooden coatrack. Jack's office had photos of extreme skiers and mountain climbers all over the walls, along with aerial maps, USGS topographicals and what appeared to be a computer printout matching topography to Global Positioning Systems coordinates.

Drawers hung slightly open on a couple of file cabinets, their contents looking ready to make a leap for it. Radio communication equipment sat on the long table behind the desk, along with a computer, fax machine and half a dozen other gadgets.

The room smelled faintly of rich cigar smoke.

She had been in Jack's office at the Denver FBI only once, but she remembered the wall full of diplomas and plaques covering a decade of service. Not one of them hung in this office.

He still had the lean body of a mountain climber, with short, curling, moonless-midnight black hair, a

Roman nose and stalwart jaw. More man than ever gave a woman much quarter. It was true then. She had been in love with Jack Slade.

She tried to suck some moisture from inside her cheeks. Swallowed. Found herself touching her short curls, all the while trying to listen, to pay attention, to concentrate on what had brought her here. To make sense of the frenzied voice crackling through the radio.

"I'm trying to tell you, Zeb. That's exactly why we launched. It's a madhouse around here, but when the officer down call came in, we ditched protocol. The call was legit, all right, but the pilot barely got off the ground before the place went up like a torch. Over."

A shrill, worried mother began leaving an insistent message that her teenage son had gone snow boarding hours ago and hadn't returned. Jack snatched up the phone and got the necessary details—name, probable location, how long "hours" really meant.

His deep, quiet, gravelly voice unstrung her. She took a step back, still shocked by the information coming through the radio. An officer down would trigger a response to the scene like no other call, but what did it mean?

Her mind raced, calculating the odds, the sheer impossibility of some other AirLife rescue followed by a different explosion than the one she had witnessed.

Neither man had yet seen her. She took a deep breath and walked into the room. "Excuse me. Jack?"

He recognized her instantly, but it took another moment to process her presence here, in Rampart, in his office. "Becky?"

She nodded, mute. Dumbstruck by the full force of his attention. Numbed by the pain in her shoulder and what she'd witnessed happening on Rabbit Foot Hill, everything seemed to fade into the background.

"What are you doing here?" He sounded harried, almost annoyed, but he hadn't taken his intensely blue eyes off her.

"I—" How did she explain in the twenty-five-words-or-less mode he seemed to expect of her? And was it her imagination or was Slade as nearly unnerved by her presence as she was by his?

On top of everything else, she thought, Zeb was finding the halting exchange between them vastly interesting, swinging his gaze from Jack to her and back again. Her taking too long to answer—or old Zeb's raised, spiky gray eyebrows—had Jack biting off his words.

"Never mind that. You'll have to wait."

Putting his call on hold, he turned to Zeb and the radio call. "They've got to be talking about the chopper I heard coming back from Willi's. An explosion would account for the blast. Find out what time this happened and where."

The old man turned to the radio. "Routt, can you give me time and place? Over."

Several long seconds passed in silence. Even the phone ceased ringing. Jack turned to the frantic mother on hold, assured her someone would go after her son as soon as possible, then rang off.

"Rampart, the log shows eleven oh five liftoff from coordinates roughly...Rabbit Foot Hill."

Jack nodded, indicating that what he heard matched the time and place in AirLife's log. Zeb frowned deeply. "Ain't anybody up there on Rabbit Foot but that crazy old Mick Hennessy."

"Yeah, well." Jack swore. "Hennessy's just loony tunes enough to shoot his grandmother if she came up his mountain and didn't properly identify herself."

"Yeah, and everybody knows that," Zeb protested. "Anyway, what's he done that a lawman'd head up there? 'Specially with a blizzard coming on?"

Jack shrugged, as if to say, "What does it matter why?" A sick, sour sensation burned her insides.

"Any possibility of survivors?"

Zeb repeated the question to the medic dispatcher on the other end into his mike. "Anyone left needs help up there? Over."

"Affirmative. Over."

Becky froze. "What does that mean?"

Zeb dutifully asked for confirmation.

"Affirmative," the Routt county dispatcher re-

peated. "At least there was before the explosion.
Hold on a minute." The disembodied voice consulted others in the background, then came back
strong. "That's right. Indications were the officer
was wounded in a shoot-out. The other guy was critically wounded, as well, but the chopper would have
had only enough space for one at a time."

She slumped in rank disbelief against Jack's desk,
staggered by the news—Watkins critically injured.

Jack gave her a sharp look. "What is it?"

"I..." Her hands began to shake. "It's just...I
can't believe this has happened. That it's over.
That..." She shrugged and shivered. "That it's even
possible."

He didn't know what she was talking about, of
course. He took the mike from Zeb and hunched
over a desk piled high with stacks of papers and
brochures he brushed aside to see yet another map.
"This is Slade, Routt Memorial. Who is the officer
down?"

"Wait a second." A long pause. "No ID yet,
Slade. Sorry. Over."

"No ID? Come on." He held the mike at a distance, muttering to Zeb.

Becky cradled her arms against herself. Jack was
perfectly justified in his incredulous doubt. In these
mountain communities, everyone knew everyone
else, with the possible exception of outlander trans-
plants who didn't count, anyway. Especially with

the level of cooperation necessary to mount even the most routine rescues.

The officer was wounded in a shoot-out. The other guy was critically wounded, as well.

Her head went light as goose-down, dizzyingly, sickeningly light. Bile washed over her tongue. She gripped the edge of the desk and made herself breathe past the bitter block in her throat.

Breathe. Just…focus.

"Come again, Routt Memorial," Jack demanded. "Was it a county or state officer? Sheriff or highway patrol?"

"None of those. What? No…check that information, Slade. We have a name. Rosen—field, Rosen—Rosen something."

Rosenberg, she thought, feeling wildly disoriented. No one but she knew that he even existed, that an FBI agent had been skiing Silver Mountain and summoned to help her.

She cleared her throat and straightened. "It's Rosenberg."

Zeb craned his neck. Jack spun around. "What did you say?"

"Rosenberg. Sam. He isn't local, Jack. He's FBI. He was here skiing—"

"Wait a minute," Jack interrupted. "Are you saying you know who's aboard that AirLife chopper?"

"Yes." She straightened. Her eyes fixed on a ruby stud in his ear. Her lips fell open, and she lost

track of what she had been going to say. The Jack
Slade she once knew would sooner neuter himself
than decorate his earlobe with a ruby stud.

But his demeanor since she'd walked into the
room contradicted whatever attitude the earring was
meant to convey—and everything she'd heard about
his go-to-hell, an-unexamined-life-is-the-only-life-
worth-leading behavior. This Slade acted the leader,
assuming command as if he had never sworn off at
all.

A man who had her respect.

A worthy man.

His eyes blazed the color blue of a gas flame. He
must have seen the possibility of admiration in her
eyes. "Stow the hero-worship and fill in the damn
blanks, Agent Difalco."

"Sorry," she snapped, embarrassed. "For a moment there I had you confused you with someone I
once admired."

He leaned on the desk, flattening his hands.
"Don't harbor any illusions, and then you won't get
confused."

She lifted her chin and blinked deliberately, refusing to be patted on the head by him, even met-
aphorically.

He glowered. "About the officer down call?"

"I don't know anything for sure," she answered
evenly. "But I missed connections with an FBI
agent this morning who may have—"

A string of obscenities crackled over the radio,

interrupting her. "Rampart, holy Jesus, are you there? Over."

"May have what?" Jack demanded, standing there hanging on to the mike.

Zeb snatched it away. "This is Rampart. What's all the hoo-ha? Over."

"They're going down. AirLife One is…" Pandemonium broke out on the other end. Shouting, confusion, a stampede of raw, frenzied, helpless swearing. "AirLife One just went down."

"Holy…no! Are you sure? Where? Over."

The answer was garbled. No worse, really, than the dispatcher trying to paste together what facts were known. Jack whipped the pencil from behind his ear and sent it crashing end over end on his desk. Both men turned all their attention to the dispatcher.

"Come again, Routt? Over."

The Routt Memorial dispatcher's report was disjointed. "Captain…SOS…no loca— Message. Still no— Emergency signal not…picked up."

Chilled, Becky ran her hands up and down her arms and approached the table behind Slade's desk. "Can they get some aircraft over the storm front to triangulate on the emergency beacon?"

"Yeah." He nodded distractedly. "But with no reliable communication, we'll have to delay until the civil air patrol can launch a flyover."

"Can you relay from radio to radio from the air patrol?"

He gave her a look that reminded her who it was she was talking to. "It's worth a shot."

"Nothing you wouldn't already have thought of, though, is it?"

His look intensified. "This is what I do, Becky." He turned to Zeb. "See if we can get word through."

Zeb rolled his eyes. The suggestion was clearly not novel to him, either. "By the way, I'm Zeb Tucker. I take it you're Becky...what was it?"

"Difalco," she said, shaking the hand he offered. "I didn't mean to insult your intelligence...."

Zeb grinned. "You couldn't, miss. But you can take a stab at Jack's all you want. One heck of a target."

"That's my ego, you old jackass," Jack snarled with obvious affection. "Suppose you round up someone to go after the missing kid and then get on the pipe and find someone to get up in the air and get those beacon coordinates."

He scribbled the name and general area in which to look for the missing teenager and handed it to Zeb, who harrumphed like a miffed old lady but turned to do as he was asked.

"Will you go?" Becky asked. "If—I mean when you get the location on the emergency beacon?"

Jack dragged a hand through his hair. He cocked his jaw as he considered what it would take. "Every rescue team within five hundred miles is tied up."

"But you'll go, won't you? There's still an officer down, a pilot, a nurse, one, at least—"

"I know the roster, Becky. But it's moot until we can pinpoint the location. That's one hell of a chore in these mountains. Even then, getting to the crash overland may be impossible."

She knew all that as well as she knew he would go after survivors if he had to crawl over some of the most rugged, ice-encrusted terrain anywhere on earth. "Take me with you."

He looked at her as if she'd just lost her last precious few brain cells. "This is out of your league, Becky."

"You're wrong," she answered steadily. "I'm certified in—"

"I know." When she thought about it, she realized he would know. Rescue teams were a pretty exclusive bunch and talked shop, exchanging stories when any two of them got together, so that, as in a mountain town, everyone knew everyone else—or had at least heard the names.

"I even believe you think you're up to this," he went on. "Terrific. You're certified. You wouldn't make the suggestion if you didn't think you were up to it. But, frankly, you'll slow me down, and I don't know what use you'd be even if you could keep up."

The problem, she thought, would not be in keeping up with Slade so much as keeping up with the overwhelming changes in her emotional landscape.

An hour ago, more like three hours now, she had been prepared to apprehend Michael Watkins in whatever manner the act required. To lie in wait and ambush him if necessary.

In the space of a heartbeat, when she saw that chopper lifting off and felt the explosion rippling through the thin mountain air with the force of a hurricane, she knew he'd escaped her. That he'd used the air ambulance to slip through her grasp as he had her father's, to perpetrate his next extortion.

And now, in another heartbeat, in some completely unforeseen twist of fate, Watkins had been defeated at the expense of the life or well-being of a man to whom the Bushwhacker was just a name in the annals of crime.

Even if the information out of Routt County was completely garbled, dead wrong, even if Watkins had played possum, escaped death, crawled away and managed to survive the brutal cold, Rosenberg had stopped him. Unlike the Unabomber, who had utilized letter bombs to carry out his carnage, Watkins's extortion demands and the explosives he used had always depended upon sophisticated remote activation.

Without his cabin, his computers, his satellite dish, and being critically wounded, Watkins had been rendered powerless.

Would he have survived the explosion? The chances against it seemed staggering. Even if he had, the blizzard had closed off the possibility of escape.

The only thing left for her to do was to assist in the rescue and pray Rosenberg had survived the assault meant for her and the crash of the AirLife chopper.

"Jack, please listen to me. It's my fault that Sam Rosenberg—"

"You said he's FBI?"

"Yes."

Jack turned to Zeb and interrupted him long enough to spit out another request. "Better find a relay to notify Denver FBI."

Zeb nodded. "Anyone else?"

"If you can get the information to Joe Aguilar at the CBI, too, that would be great."

Zeb turned to the radio and began working on it. Jack sat there looking at her.

She waited, expecting him to ask her how she fit into the disaster on Rabbit Foot Hill. He outwaited her. The place was far from quiet. The phone rang again. Another message, another stranded motorist being reported. Zeb sat pulling his hair out, on the radio tracking down any information he could get that would pinpoint the AirLife crash.

Still, the silence between them lengthened awkwardly.

"Aren't you going to ask me how I'm responsible for dragging Rosenberg into this?"

He cut her a look. "A secret tryst?"

She stared at him. Was he completely oblivious to her? Had he always been? "Yeah," she agreed, wallowing in sarcasm, "that's it."

His eyes narrowed. "That's not exactly a denial."

"It wouldn't be any of your business, either. I'm talking about—"

"Look, Becky, I don't want to know what you're talking about."

"I don't believe that." She did believe him, of course, but maybe he could be provoked into stepping up to the plate. "Even you—"

"Even *less*," he interrupted, "if it has anything to do with running some scum bag felon to ground." He met her gaze straight on, unflinching, unrepentant, not quite uncaring. "Whatever you were doing here, whatever Rosenberg was doing, whatever the hell Mick Hennessy did or did not do to invite your attention has zilch to do with any rescue attempt on that crash site. Are you tracking this?"

"No problem."

She got it loud and clear. If he wanted to think the life-and-death responsibilities of mountain rescues were different than the crisis that had made him turn his back on law enforcement, let him. They weren't. Not really. He preferred some macho man-against-nature contest over a man-against-man one.

He might delude himself. He didn't fool her. He

was riddled with latent heroic tendencies he couldn't escape. But she knew what he meant.

Clearly.

She lobbed the truth out there to see if he would recognize it. Was Jack Slade really too far gone to give a simple damn?

"You wouldn't care if I had the drop on Michael Watkins, would you?"

He surprised her a little. Not because he gave a serious or second thought to whether she had Watkins dead to rights or not, but because he didn't congratulate her within a split second for catching his drift.

"I might care, Becky." Surprising her again. He looked away and dragged his fingers down muscles and tendons in the back of his neck.

She knew he knew what impact Watkins had had on her family.

"It's just not my gig anymore," he went on finally. "I'm not excusing myself, explaining, rationalizing or apologizing. I'm stating a simple matter of fact. And I'd rather not spend any more valuable time correcting whatever lingering and misguided sentiments as to my character you may still be nursing along."

"Trust me, Jack, I've not a single illusion left where you're concerned." If anything, she was seeing beyond the facade of fickleness and irresponsibility he was so invested in projecting. "But you're absolutely right. It doesn't really matter why I came." It mattered a great deal to her that Watkins had been stopped, and to his intended victims, but her mission in Rampart wasn't the issue anymore.

"The point is that I'm here, you could use the help, and I'm qualified in mountain rescue. In short, if you're going, I'm going with you."

He shook his beautifully shaped head. "No way. Remember the very first rule of mountain rescue? There's one man in charge. That would be me. That means I have final say, which means I decide who goes and who doesn't."

"Of course. But—" She broke off.

Why should she argue with Jack over this when she was clearly in territory he had mastered far more than she ever would? Because if Sam Rosenberg had taken down Michael Watkins at the risk of his own life, then she owed him a debt of gratitude she could never begin to repay.

No. Her undying gratitude might be appreciated, but it wouldn't really make any difference to Rosenberg. The risks came with the job of taking the predators and criminals down.

She felt uneasy, jittery. As if more depended on getting Jack to agree to take her than she knew was at stake. She'd been tossed from pillar to post by events in the past twenty-four hours, happenings fraught with conflicting implications.

She had to go, had to convince Jack to take her, whether she understood her own motives or not.

He handled another call for assistance, then folded his arms across his chest. "I'm listening, Becky, but as you can tell, I have my hands full without haggling over a nonissue with you."

Chapter Four

"All right." She stuffed her uneasiness. "If I can't keep up, you'll know it inside an hour, and you can just send me back, no argument."

"We're talking *days*, Becky, not hours. Not an hour. I don't have the manpower to initiate a rescue in the first place. There's sure as hell not going to be anyone to come after you when you fall behind."

"I won't fall behind."

"I have no way of knowing that, Becky, and I'm not going to risk—"

"Call up Bob Pinkie, then." Pinkie directed the Rocky Mountain Rescue volunteers out of Boulder County where she had trained and served on a couple of treacherous rescue missions. "Bob will vouch for me."

"He might if he could come to the phone. If the phone lines were operational. If Rocky Mountain wasn't already fully deployed themselves." He held up a finger and listened to an incoming message canceling a couple of calls, then gave her a dismissive shrug. "Becky, look. If I can't muster a six-man stretcher team and at least two relief carriers, then there's no point in anyone going out but me."

"That's not true," she returned, certain at least of this territory. "You can't evacuate anyone without a stretcher team, so the point of going out at all is to provide life support until you can muster teams to evacuate the victims. And if there is more than one survivor in a crash like that, then two hands are nowhere near enough to cope with the life support."

Zeb turned. Rubbing his jaw, he put in his two cents. "She's got you there, boss."

Jack tossed Zeb a quelling, implacable look. He would not be second-guessed, and every comeback she made or Zeb tossed in only served to make Jack dig in his heels. Before he could do that, she took another tack.

"Okay, Jack. If taking me is really against your better judgment, then that's the way it will be. I can't get out of Rampart, but I'm sure I can pitch in and help somewhere. I don't want to compromise the chances of any of the AirLife crew, or Rosenberg, for that matter."

He took a deep breath and quieted. She might have made the right decision. Acquiescing seemed to get her more consideration than any argument she had made.

He looked her up and down, reluctantly assessing her strength. "How much weight can you manage?"

"Sixty pounds. Seventy."

He cocked his head, seeming, at least, to be thinking of the possibilities over the drawbacks. "I assume you're also trained in survival?"

"Of course."

"Do you have your gear with you? Boots? Snowshoes?"

"Always. I'd like to go buy a few things, but it won't take me more than an hour."

"All right." He stood. Zeb gave her a wink behind Jack's back. "You can come along. If you can hold your own and you know what you're doing when we get there, then another pair of hands might make a difference. But crash survivors get first priority, Becky, so you'd better get yourself prepared to survive on your own, because I *will* leave you behind if it comes to that."

She nodded. Uncertainty thumped inside her. The nerve of it, the extremes in weather and mobility she would face, and face with an uncompromising partner. "You won't regret it, Jack. Is there anything you need while I'm at it?"

"Thanks, but no."

BUT HE DID. Checking his gear with more vigor than was strictly necessary, Jack knew what he needed was to have his head examined. Bob Pinkie could vouch for her six ways from Sunday. She might be the finest, most adept, courageous, persistent, dogged, never-say-die rescue personnel on the planet. The fact was, he already knew all that, and it didn't change the unhappy fact that her voice alone gave him a stiff, savage jolt in the groin.

He knew exactly what his problem was. The forbidden fruit, more or less. He'd met Becky Difalco four years ago in the autumn, in Denver, when the aspen went gold, the fire bushes turned a brilliant scarlet and the nights grew cool. The occasion was an interagency volleyball game at Congress Park.

She was a player. A tall, pale, dark-haired beauty. Lithe. Strong enough to go the distance, sexy enough between the halter top she wore, the beads of sweat that gathered between her breasts and her kick-ass smile to more than pique his interest.

She'd looked at him often enough that day to suggest she was available for a casual flirtation, as well. But weeks later, he knew he'd gone beyond the point of anything even remotely casual in his feelings for her.

Problem was, Becky turned out to be the de facto little sister to the whole damn law enforcement community in Colorado. What had happened to her, surviving the blast that destroyed her childhood home and killed her mother, costing her, as well, her father as she once knew him, was every cop's version of hell on earth. Any man with an interest in Becky had better come hat in hand, honorable intentions in plain view, because said suitor became instantly answerable to a couple of hundred cops-cum-thugs.

She'd broken it off. He'd thought at the time it was just as well. The terms had scared him spitless.

Still did.

He examined his boots, his backpack, the batteries in the handheld GPS, the ignition on the miniature butane torch. He folded and packed his sleeping gear, climbing apparatus, pitons, the charges necessary for avalanche control, a variety of flares, then the life-support equipment.

The mental checklist went on. The preparations got done, and all the while he assured himself that she was no more or less to him than any other member of any other rescue crew. That this wasn't about wanting sex with her despite how exquisitely her voice strummed his lust.

He knew better, no doubt. In the process of a search-and-rescue mission in the middle of a blizzard, he was not likely to cave in to his baser instincts. Or even come close, even think about Becky Difalco that way.

What he feared, what he most needed his head examined for was that he didn't know how he was going to deal with her misplaced faith in his higher nature.

That she refused to take him at his word—not his authority, but his self-characterization. That she listened to him tell her it wasn't his gig anymore to care if she had the notorious Bushwhacker in her sights and refused to believe him.

That she would stand up to his smart-ass, uncalled-for remarks about shacking up with Rosenberg.

That she had the feminine nerve, or guilelessness, to let it show she was still half in love with him.

And finally that, when the first hint of hero worship lit up in her doe brown eyes, he found himself wanting to live up to higher expectations. Like being true to himself first. Like embracing truth and fidelity and freedom and justice for all, amen. Like he hadn't gone completely to the dogs.

Like owning up to the fact that he was still half in love with her.

He knew one thing. He didn't need or want to measure up, because if you once let yourself live by the sword, you inevitably died by it, as well. Thirty pairs of innocent, terrified eyes didn't lie, and Jack Slade was no hero.

He liked his unregenerate life-style just fine. As with this rescue, he even saved a few endangered lives here and there to weigh in his favor—just in case it turned out there was a heaven and hell with some archangel type in charge of assignments one way or the other.

He began hauling equipment to his Explorer and put the dilemma to rest. He intended to live hard and die young. And when he wound up falling well short of Becky Difalco's romantic notions of who he was, she wouldn't be able to say he hadn't warned her.

HE LEFT at one-thirty, still without word on where the AirLife chopper had gone down. He towed a couple of cars out of hip-high snowdrifts and then drove to the general store to pick up extra rations and butane.

Gunnar Schmit had been left to run the place on his own, which was a real stretch. He'd shown Jack more of the high-country nooks and crannies and dangers than any half-dozen other men. Gunnar had lived and hiked, skiied and explored these mountains his entire life, so his command of his environs was to be expected. If he could handle a Sno-Cat, he could surely operate the simple cash register. But a crowd was more than he could deal with.

It looked as though Gunnar wanted to drop everything and talk to Jack, which would have really hacked off the customers impatiently waiting to make their purchases and get home before the roads got completely impassable.

Jack waved at Gunnar, who shouted, "Wait! Jack! Wait!" as if Jack were heading out the door instead of picking up what he wanted. He collected the items, went to the counter and dropped a fifty, trying to get by with giving the guy an encouraging thumbs-up. "Keep the change, Gunnar."

"Keep the change...no, but wait!" He started to come out from behind the counter.

Shirley, the morning waitress from the truck stop, reached her beefy fist out and grabbed Gunnar by the ear to steer him behind the cash register. "You lookit here, you bum—"

"You bum," he repeated anxiously, knocking her

arm away. "Just take it, just take it. Jack, tell 'em to just take the stuff!"

Tempted to grab Gunnar by his orange and blue plaid collar and tell him to shape up, Jack heaved a sigh and lived up to another set of expectations he'd dump if he had the sense God gave a goose. Shifting his load, he pulled out a wad of fifty-dollar bills from his money clip and tossed them into the open drawer of the cash register.

"There. That should cover everything. Everybody just sack up what you've got and clear out."

He took Gunnar aside while the locals hustled their stuff into bags and got out before he came to his senses and took the wad of fifties back.

"Okay. What is it, Gunnar?"

"Okay. Okay." He gulped in some air. "Mick's place—"

"I know," Jack interrupted gently. He blew out a frustrated breath. He didn't have time to deal with this.

"Mick's dead, Gunnar. I'm sorry. AirLife took out—"

"Mick's dead, Mick's dead. No. He can't be," Gunnar denied heatedly, gripping Jack's arm.

"Yeah, Gunnar, he is. He popped off and shot at an FBI agent—"

"Shot an FBI agent," he repeated robotlike, but his face mottled with anger. "Nope. No way. It's on account a that girl. It's that girl," Gunnar shouted. "She's bad news, Jack. *Bad* news. Bad news."

Jack groaned. It didn't take much imagination to link Gunnar's version of bad news with Becky Difalco. "Look. Could you let go of my arm?" Gunnar moved his hand, which went right away into a fist. Jack went on. "You know Mick's loaded for bear. He's fired on people before—"

"Fired on people..." Gunnar flushed angrily. "That's a lie. Nobody hardly ever even sees Mick. When's the last time you seen Mick? Who's ever gone to the sheriff?"

"What does that have to do with anything, Gunnar?" Jack interrupted, shaking his head. Because no one had ever pressed charges against Hennessy—probably out of fear that the recluse was unbalanced enough to track them down and do the job right—didn't mean Hennessy hadn't taken potshots at trespassers.

Gunnar's blind loyalty to anyone who treated him with a little humanity was one of his more endearing qualities, but not at the moment. "Do you see that, Gunnar? You don't fire on a cop. You can't even point a loaded weapon at a cop and not be in a boatload of trouble."

"Mick's smart," he answered stonily. "Nobody could beat him. Mick's like that, Jack. You know. Mick's way too smart, 'n' if he—"

"Gunnar, calm down." Why now? Why me? would have been a better question, except that Jack hadn't ever brushed Gunnar off as if the poor guy didn't exist. "This is me—Jack. I'm your friend. I tell you the truth, now, don't I? Haven't I always told you the truth?"

"Always told you the truth," Gunnar admitted, but his fists closed tighter.

"Look, buddy. I don't know exactly what happened, and I haven't got the time right now to explain, even if I did. You gotta handle the store, though, and right now I've got to go out on a rescue."

Gunnar's cheeks puffed out in a menacing look. "She's got a gun, Jack. Girl's bad news and she's got a gun. Got a gun. I seen it."

"I know, Gunnar." He didn't know, but he believed Gunnar because he was probably incapable of making up things like that. It wasn't unusual for a CBI agent to carry. But unless Becky was one hell of a dangerous renegade and a liar, as well, which Jack didn't believe at all, Gunnar had things badly confused. "I'll take care of it, okay? She's assisting on the rescue. She won't even be around. Will you trust me to take care of it? I'm asking as your friend now."

Gunnar nodded at length.

Jack didn't intend to take care of it. Saying he would was probably a shit-heel thing to do, playing on Gunnar's trust. Especially since it didn't matter to Jack one way or another that she was armed. Still, he couldn't waste any more time, so he justified the expedient promise.

"That's my man. You take care of things around here now, okay?"

Gunnar swallowed hard. Jack could see a lingering doubt in his wide-set eyes. "Take care of things around here. Sure nuf."

WHEN JACK finally got into his vehicle, Zeb was on the radio trying to raise him.

He picked up the mike. "Slade here, Rampart. What's going on? Over," he added wearily.

"Where the dickens you been? Over."

"Zeb?" He let a sufficiently long silence go by to make his point. "What do you have?"

"Got lucky," Zeb answered snappily, having divined the twilight zone of Jack's tolerance for pointless explanations. "The air patrol was able to detail a flyover. We've got longitude and latitude from triangulating on the emergency beacon from the AirLife crash site. Over. Oh, and Miss Difalco says to tell you she's ready whenever you are. Over again."

"Thanks." Smart-aleck woman. He should have sent her for the supplies when she offered. "I'm on my way."

Within ten minutes, he met her in his office and matched the location the air patrol had triangulated on, pinpointing the expected location of the crash site on the wall map. Becky studied the surrounding terrain on the relief map while Jack tested his accuracy against a computer program designed to nail down the coordinates with the geographic features.

She frowned. In triangulating on the beacon, she knew, the readings came off an automatic direction finder. At a point where two or more plotted lines intersected, they would find the helicopter's emergency locator transmitter. But in degrees north and south, east and west, not accounting for the mountains. "What about the altitude of the crash site? How do you know that?"

"We don't." Jack stood behind her while the computer churned through its extensive calculations. Her short cap of shiny deep brown curls smelled faintly of an almond-scented shampoo. "We can make a fairly decent guess, though, and plug the coordinates, longitude and latitude, into a GPS."

She stood squarely in front of the yellow pushpin marking the expected coordinates. Otherwise, when he circumscribed the search area with his finger, he wouldn't have had to reach over her shoulder.

She peered at the topographical map. "You're thinking a circle with a radius of a quarter mile?"

He shrugged. "Better than throwing a dart. Look at this." He began closing in on the site with his finger. Skittish, she moved a little to the side. "The terrain is rugged, but worse, the vertical drop is staggering. The chopper could be somewhere near the top of this peak, which is thirteen-five-fifty in altitude, to as far down as this valley, which is, say, a thousand feet lower but still within the search radius.''

''Then it could as easily be the other side of the peak.''

He nodded. ''Now you see what I mean. The ordinary search and rescues involve hikers or skiers who inadvertently wandered off a proscribed trail. This is a different ball of wax.''

The computer beeped, signaling a completed task. Jack turned and examined the screen. ''Looks like we have our work cut out for us.''

''Hey, Jack!'' A lanky teenage boy came spilling into the room and grabbed a set of headphones.

Concentrating on the computer screen, Jack barely glanced up. ''Hey, kid.''

The boy gave Becky a curious look. She started to wave, but a couple of phone lines rang at once and he took off to catch the calls.

Turning her attention to the computer, she watched over Jack's shoulder, trying to match the split-screen topographical map with the elevation map, which looked more like a crude drawing of the mountains from the viewpoint of an artist on the ground. Small circles within circles, like an archer's target, marked the computer's estimate of location.

''How did the program decide that the crash site is on this side of the peak rather than the other?''

''I fed in the last known flight path. Assuming that the chopper was heading to Steamboat Springs, from here, at Rabbit Foot Hill, the pilot would have taken this north-northwesterly route.''

''Which means what, exactly? Unless the chopper crashed into the mountain—''

''We know it didn't, or the pilot wouldn't have had time to blink, much less put in a distress call.''

''Then the fact that the helicopter went down on the far side means it cleared the peak?''

''Possibly.'' He nodded. ''But look. Where the computer placed the target is only the mathematical probability ranging from here—'' he clicked the mouse and put up a tiny circle with a cross in it ''—to here.'' He clicked the computer mouse again at the other end. The program graphics translated the markers into their relative positions on the other side of the split screen. He sent the mouse sailing to a print option.

''That's it. That's our destination.''

Whatever experience she'd had didn't begin to address decisions like these. ''Where do we start?''

He took the page off the printer as it rolled out, then pointed to a spot on the topographical map. ''Here. This is the closest trailhead.'' He looked at his watch. ''It's five-twenty. If we leave now, we'll make it by, say, nine or ten o'clock tonight, which means we can really get started at sunup tomorrow.''

She'd expected as much. Every hour spent counted against any survivors. ''Can you drive as far as the trailhead?''

"We're going to try. We'll switch over to the snowmobile when we can't get any farther. From there, though, we'll be on foot."

He took her by the shoulders. "Don't take this personally. I mean that. But this will be the hardest thing you've ever done in your life. Now is the time to say so if you have any doubts at all."

He'd already gone over all her purchases to satisfy himself that she was well outfitted. This was a question of her stamina, and he had a right, an obligation, really, to ask at every juncture until they departed the targeted trailhead.

Maybe he was overdoing it just a little.

"I am as well prepared for this as anyone short of a professional." She added, "I don't intimidate easily, Jack."

"I knew that before you walked in the door."

He looked steadily at her, his eyes conveying an unforeseen regard for her. But tingeing the esteem, something nearer a masculine warning hovered. Something less for the sake of her safety and well-being and more…predatory.

Male to female.

A wayward thrill spread across her breasts, up her neck beneath her slate gray cotton turtleneck. She'd fantasized such a moment for so long and thought it so unlikely. Her pulse skipped.

She wondered distractedly what he knew or thought he knew. Whether his grudging respect sprang from things she considered important or whether it didn't. How ironic that the flame blue color of his eyes should remind her…fighting fire with fire was sometimes even more dangerous than playing with it.

And how implausibly senseless it was to respond as a woman, anyway. "Are you flirting with me, Jack?"

"If I were…" He paused. She thought he was going to say, *If I were, you wouldn't have to ask,* and then she'd just have to die. He took unconscionably long to go on. "Maybe I should say, if I am flirting with you, Becky, I'd be disappointed if you fell for it."

She straightened. "So would I."

"Then we understand each other?"

"Perfectly." She thought she pulled that off nicely, but what hope was there when, even in the thick of powerful, conflicting emotions and doubts over Michael Watkins's fate, she could be distracted by her attraction to Slade?

He looked away, then crossed his arms over his chest. "Why is it that I'm not convinced?"

"Because you're insufferable and you think you know everything?" she snapped. He started to grin. She snatched her parka off the coat tree. "I'm serious, Jack. Yes, all right! I'm attracted to you—"

"I knew it."

"—against overwhelming odds, I might add. This is way too much. What do you want from me?"

"The truth is all. I'll put this as plainly as I know

how. I haven't even pulled off a search and rescue attempt like this myself. I have to be able to count on you, just like you have to trust me absolutely."

"Will you be needing a sworn affidavit that I won't jeopardize the rescue and try to seduce you in the middle of a damn blizzard? Or are you worried that I'll push you off some cliff because you rejected me?" He didn't offer to interrupt her, but his lips twitched.

"I can just hear it now," she went on, wound up, mimicking the sensationalism of a teaser for the TV news. "This just in! Spurned female CBI agent, rendered mindless by unrequited love, deep-sixes offending doofus ski bum and scuttles mountain rescue efforts! Details on the ten o'clock news."

He broke out laughing. "Mindless? Really? Damn. I must be better than I thought."

"No."

"No?"

"No." She couldn't help cracking a smile, too. "You're just the doofus." But the I-am-an-idiot-aren't-I? look on his face threw her for a loop. "I think the real truth is that you're scared to death."

He scoffed. "Of what?"

"Blowing your act."

"What act would that be?"

"That you don't care about anything important—"

"I don't."

"—most of all whether the bad guys get what's

coming to them.'' She shook her hair and plunged ahead before he could interrupt. ''That you're just as attracted to me as I am to you—''

He sighed.

She gulped. ''Don't bother denying it, Jack.''

''Becky—''

''Forget it, Jack! I don't believe you! It's meaningless. Nothing is going to happen between us, but if you weren't attracted to me, you wouldn't even see a problem. You could ignore me, pat me on the head, treat me like a sister—or worse. One of the guys.

''But most of all—'' she jammed her hands into synthetic, wicking-liner gloves for emphasis, awed that she had managed to wipe the smugly assured mirth right off his altogether too incredibly good-looking face ''—you're scared that you might actually show up behaving like the guy I might really have cared about. Only then it will be too late.''

''Damn.'' He blew out a breath. He'd bullied the truth out of her on the pretext of the integrity of the rescue mission. He didn't have the nerve to stand there and deny a single charge. ''You're better than I thought, too.''

She poked her chin up. ''Thank you.''

''You're welcome.''

Chapter Five

He had nothing to say to her on the drive up the pass to the trailhead. She would have liked to believe his silence had to do with calling him on his act and doing it well, but it wasn't likely. The twisting, torturous mountain highway—what there was to imagine of it beneath the drifts of snow—required his total concentration. At near-zero visibility, he had only the intermittent road reflectors to gauge his progress.

The swirling cocoon of snow in the headlights against the black of night closed in from every direction, forcing a strained sort of intimacy. If she'd been alone, a certain level of uneasiness approaching panic would have set in by now. As it was, the emotional tension between them lingered like the scent of frost in the air, and the grim set of Jack's jaw didn't do much to instill confidence in their physical safety.

She wished for any other circumstances but these to have met up with Slade again. In another setting, his me-first, let-the-devil-take-the-hindmost attitude would have stamped paid to her lingering attraction to him. She could have seen Slade the way he wanted to be seen, disdained him, given him up for a lost cause.

If the space in the Explorer weren't so over-whelmingly *his*. So taken up with his brawn and red-bloodedness, with the rich and obnoxious scent of his cigars, which she had yet to see him pull out. With the glint of light off the in-your-face, take-it-or-leave-it ruby stud in his earlobe…if he'd looked like, say, Gunnar Schmit, she would have been safe.

She didn't feel safe.

She knew why. Instead of showing up like the thrill-seeking doofus ski bum performing some ex-traordinary feat of derring-do, Jack Slade was prob-ably going to prove his true colors, showing up as the kind of man she could well and truly love, and her crush on him would only deepen.

Give it up, she commanded herself. She was as safe as she needed to be. It didn't matter. She could admire his staggering good looks, his ruggedness, even his ability to rise to the occasion once in a while without sacrificing her heart or her good sense. Crushes were for schoolgirls, and happily ever afters for fairy tales.

She reached to turn down the heater. A pain shot through her shoulder where she'd fallen hours ago. She must have flinched, but a quick glance made her think he hadn't noticed. "You're squinting. Are you doing okay?"

"Yeah." He rubbed each eye in turn with the heel of his left hand. "Thanks for asking."

"You're welcome."

She thought he might take the opening to talk, maybe ramble to fill the silence. When he didn't, she gave up and returned her thoughts to Rabbit Foot Hill, and what it meant.

Part of her wanted to let go, to numb out, accept the relief and elation of believing that Michael Watkins had been stopped. She wanted to believe so much that she couldn't think straight. The threat he posed had been so uppermost in her thoughts for the last few weeks that her mind seemed to stand still at the unrecognizable abyss.

If Sam Rosenberg had taken Michael Watkins down in a shoot-out on Rabbit Foot Hill, the FBI agent would become an instant celebrity. A hero with all the acclaim her father had ever wanted.

If it was true, she wanted none of the glory, not even a footnote. All she wished for was to spare more innocent lives. To save the inevitable survivors the grief of a lifetime.

But a scenario in which Michael Watkins was already dead—handily, simply defeated—felt like Pollyanna thinking. If he could be so easily dispatched, then she'd been shadowboxing a figment of her imagination. Tracking down a paper tiger. Seeing ghosts where there was only an incompetent old man.

The Bushwhacker was not a figment of anyone's imagination, and she didn't trust a neat and tidy resolution that wrapped up the saga of the Bushwhacker and turned Sam Rosenberg into a wounded hero—assuming he lived to tell the story at all.

Her natural tendency to expect that things would always, finally, go wrong nagged at her. It appeared that just this once, events had finally gone terribly wrong not for her, but for her father's nemesis. Expecting to confront Louis Difalco's daughter, Watkins had been caught off guard by Rosenberg. Maybe Watkins was dead and gone, nothing more than a ghost left for her to excise from her heart.

But the explosion raised her doubts.

If Watkins was dead when the AirLife helicopter lifted off, who triggered the blast? The only answer that made sense was that Watkins had survived the gun battle. He would have had to assume she was still out there somewhere as backup to Rosenberg. Forced to improvise, she reasoned, he was fully capable of touching off an explosion of the propane tank that would kill two birds with one stone. Whatever evidence against him still in existence would be destroyed. At the same time, the conflagration would create the diversion he desperately needed to slip away from her—or convince her he could not have escaped alive.

Startling her out of her reverie, Jack groped for

the thermos on the seat beside him and held it out to her, never taking his eyes off the illusion of a highway. "Pour me some coffee, would you?"

She took the thermos and unscrewed the cup. "How much farther?"

He glanced at the odometer. "The turnoff should be coming up in a few minutes."

She poured the coffee, tucked the thermos between her legs and handed him the cup. "Is there a sign indicating the trailhead?"

"Yeah. You'll see it on the left, probably about two seconds before the turn." He took a swallow of coffee and made a grateful noise. "Thank God Jill is taking care of the coffee. Zeb couldn't make a decent pot to save his soul."

"Who's Jill?"

"Jill Gaylor. Slade's Adventures receptionist, secretary, gofer. She also mans the phones and radio—most of the time—and dispatches the rescue teams."

"Where was she earlier?"

"There was apparently some pregnant woman stranded on a road to one of the local ranches. There wasn't anyone else to go and no other woman on the ranch." He took another swallow. "Jill's son, Randy, was the kid handling the phones when we left."

"That's a lot of responsibility for a boy that age."

"Yeah. Probably. But kids live up to amazing responsibility when the chips are down."

She allowed herself a smile in the dark. "Careful, Jack. Your humanity is showing."

He gave her a look. "Randy's a great kid, and it's not like there was a whole lot of choice. Besides, Zeb was out at the hangar."

She let a few moments pass. Let him off the hook, or herself. Her nerves, she knew, had as much to do with being alone in the dark with him as with the driving conditions—or the possibility the Bushwhacker had found a way to survive.

She wouldn't believe until she saw for herself, with her own eyes, that Watkins was dead. All her fears grounded themselves in the likelihood that he was not. That he had escaped, not cleanly, not sufficiently to perpetrate his terrorist plans, but alive. She shivered, suffering the notion that she should have gone after him and let Jack take this mission on alone, as he'd wanted.

"What's going on in that head of yours?" he asked.

In no uncertain terms, he'd let her know he didn't really want to know where her thoughts and intentions were or what they had been in coming to Rampart. She answered the inconsequential question she thought he was asking. "I was deciding that you didn't want to talk and drive through this whiteout at the same time."

He shook his head briefly. "If I need you to be quiet, I'll let you know." She saw the trailhead marker after he eased off on the gas pedal and handed her the thermos cup. "This is it. Finish that, will you, so it doesn't slop on your hands."

He slowed to a crawl, downshifted and turned. She gulped the rest of the coffee, bidding her no-caffeine campaign goodbye, and braced herself.

He took the drive in low gear, slow and steady. The road cut a narrow swath through the thick forest. "You want to talk about it?"

She gave a quick glance at him. His focus was fixed on the road. "What?"

"What's bothering you."

Remind him, she thought. "I don't think you want to hear about it, Jack."

"Probably not." He shrugged, then gave her an unnervingly long look considering that he needed to be watching the twists and turns. "It's not that I don't care, Becky."

The master of mixed messages. "If it would help, spit it out."

"Okay. I'm concerned about the explosion that happened as AirLife lifted off the ground."

"What about it?"

"I was there." More than that, she thought. What if she was wrong and Watkins had the wherewithal to carry out one final act of terrorism meant to rub her nose in her incompetence? But she left that unsaid.

"You saw it?"

"Yes."

"Was it the propane tank that blew?"

"I think so, but it happened so fast. It must have been, though."

"Okay. So you were there. What happened?"

"I don't know. That's just the problem. I heard the helicopter coming, but I was on foot. It took me a long time to make it up the mountain, and by the time I got there, AirLife was lifting off, and a split second later, the explosion came."

He slowed at a turnoff she would never have suspected was there. The Explorer jolted down a steep embankment, then climbed through snowdrifts deep enough to bury a small car. The trailer carrying the snowmobile clanked and groaned, but the heavy snow muted even that noise. Finally a small, primitive cabin came into view.

"The Trailhead Hilton," Jack announced, stopping the vehicle. "We'll spend the night here."

"Separate accommodations, I presume."

"Yeah, with your very own hot tub, masseur and fresh strawberries."

"Jack, you're such a considerate host." She had expected to be pitching a tent.

Cracking a smile, he rolled his eyes and shut off the ignition. He had to shove several times against the snowdrift outside the door to create a wedge large enough to squeak his body through. The sub-zero cold invaded the interior so fast her exhalations began forming small clouds.

She drew on her gloves, pulled a woolen mask over her face and opened her own door, making her own wedge. Jack was already around to her side, jerking the door open and stomping down the drifts so she wouldn't have to wade through waist-high snow.

Turning in her seat, she hefted her backpack, then wriggled through the door and dragged her pack with her. She slung one strap over her shoulder and followed close behind Jack as he churned a path to the door.

He opened the unlocked door and shone the flashlight around the inside of the cabin. In the summer season the small log building served as a way station and had a communications board where hikers could indicate when they'd taken off and when they expected to return. There wasn't a stick of furniture save a small potbellied wood-burning stove.

"Do you have what you need for the night in your pack?"

Becky pulled off her mask and nodded. "Yes. Do we need to bring anything in?"

"There's a partial cord of firewood to the right side of the steps." He clanked open the stove door and directed the beam of the flashlight into the stove. Making sure, Becky thought, that no critters had taken up residence. "I'll haul in a couple of armloads if you want to get my bedroll."

"Deal."

She replaced her mask and headed out the door with his keys in hand to open the back window of the Explorer. The cold was no deeper outside the cabin than in, but the biting wind felt as though it had frozen a chunk out of her lungs before she got back with his thermos and bedroll. Jack collected split logs, banged the snow off them and brought in enough to warm the cabin.

He shucked his hat, coat and gloves and set the logs in the stove. Becky unstuffed her sleeping bag and spread it out close behind Jack.

"Do you want the rest of the coffee while it's still warm?"

"Thanks, yeah."

Still bundled up, she sat cross-legged on her sleeping bag and poured coffee.

He splintered one of the logs with his bare hands and tossed the kindling beneath the logs, then reached for his coat. He retrieved a penlike butane torch from a breast pocket, took the cup of luke-warm coffee and squatted at the stove door to start the fire.

Only the tiny hiss of butane disturbed the frozen silence till the kindling started to crackle. The cold penetrated to her bones, and she shivered hard. Her teeth began to chatter.

He stared at the flames taking hold. "Relax, Becky."

"I'm trying, Jack." She shivered violently. "Don't worry about it. Once we're moving, I'll be fine."

He reached again for his coat and took a small

silver flask from a pocket. He handed it to her, offering her a sip. "This will help."

"What is it?"

"Brandy."

She knew the liquor would fill her with the sensation of warmth, enough maybe to convince her body to relax. "Thanks."

She twisted off the cap and took a small sip, savoring the hot, exquisite taste on her tongue, then swallowed and sipped again. Heat spread through her as if the brandy had gone straight to her veins. Her shivering stopped as suddenly as it had come on. "This is really, really good."

"Should be. It's a Reserve."

"Do you want a swig?"

"No. Thanks." He rolled the last of the coffee around the bottom of the cup and tossed it down. Still squatting by the fire, rubbing his hands together, Jack watched her uncrimp herself. "That's all there is, so conserve."

She nodded and screwed the cap on.

"So." He returned to their interrupted conversation. "Within seconds of AirLife getting off the ground, the explosion went off. What did you think happened?"

"I thought at the time that the—that he'd gotten away." There was no overwhelming reason not to say Watkins's name aloud. Or the Bushwhacker. Still, she didn't. "That he'd called in AirLife for himself and slipped through my fingers."

He took out a cigar, unwrapped it, bit off the end. He didn't ask if she minded, didn't even cast an inquiring look her way. "You're the one who told us it was Rosenberg."

"I know." Shivering hard, she held her hands toward the stove. "When I came into your office, the radio dispatcher was saying they'd scrapped protocol and launched the chopper only because the call was for an officer down. I was in shock, Jack. I had no idea Rosenberg had gone up there, but if AirLife had launched in response to an officer down, then it had to be Rosenberg."

Jack frowned. "So you went from believing that your perp had escaped to believing it must be Rosenberg instead. Now you think AirLife was mistaken?"

"Not exactly." She took a deep breath, exhaled, then began to clarify. "I told you I'd missed connections with him, which is true. But I've never even met Sam Rosenberg, and I don't know if he thought I was going to meet him on Rabbit Foot Hill."

"Maybe Rosenberg figured something had happened to you up there."

She hesitated. "I hadn't thought of that, but it makes sense. If he thought I was in trouble, then he would have gone up to check it out, if nothing else."

Jack expelled a rush of smoke. "How is it that you didn't have confirmed backup?"

"Because when I came up here, I didn't know

what I was going to find. Or who. When I knew what I was dealing with, I called Joe Aguilar, but by then, the roads were closed and no one could get to Rampart. Joe said he'd run it by the Denver FBI and see if there wasn't some way to get backup in.

"He e-mailed me later that Rosenberg was already in the valley on a skiing trip. The phone lines must have gone down in the middle of the transmission, because I didn't get a time or place to meet with him."

"So you went alone."

His tone irritated her. "Don't judge me, Jack. I had my reasons."

"I'm sure you did."

She broke off, meeting his eyes, saying nothing, refusing to justify herself to a man who, whatever his inescapable heroic proclivities, had walked away from it all.

He jabbed at the burning logs with the branch he'd been using for a poker. "How did Rosenberg know where to go?"

"I had learned about Rabbit Foot Hill when I called Joe yesterday afternoon. He would have given the FBI all the information I gave him."

"Becky, I still have no idea where you're going with this," he said after a few minutes.

She straightened and scraped a hand through her hair. "Okay. I originally thought the guy I was after had escaped on the chopper. But we know it was

Rosenberg, so my guy cannot have escaped. At least not on that chopper.''

"Okay. Assume for a moment that it was Rosenberg the AirLife crew picked up. What then?''

"Then my guy was left for dead, and there's the possibility that he wasn't. That he survived, and now he's getting away.''

"Even if he is alive, Becky, he won't get far. Not in this blizzard.''

"I know. But with this guy, Jack, that's small comfort.''

"Are you second-guessing yourself?''

"About?''

"Coming on this rescue instead of going after Hennessy?''

"Yes.'' The simple omission of Watkins's name in her story became a more insidious lie the moment Jack called him Hennessy, as if that was the man she believed herself to be pursuing. She let it ride, telling herself Jack didn't want the truth when in reality, she needed the emotional distance from Jack that confiding in him would confuse.

He remained silent for a long time.

"Are you worried that I really won't have the mental focus to go ahead with the rescue?''

"Will you?''

"Yes.'' She rested an elbow on her knee, her chin on the backs of her fingers. "Jack, are you second-guessing yourself in bringing me along? Because we've covered that territory, too.''

"Yeah. We have." The wood fire mostly consumed the scent of the cigar smoke. He sank to the cold, scarred wooden floor, then settled back, leaning on his elbows, taking a drag off the cigar. His jaw tilted. In the firelight she watched his throat muscles tighten, his lips forming smoke rings that wavered toward the ceiling. The crease between his eyes deepened.

"Then what? What are you thinking?"

"I'm thinking I don't understand what made you go after Hennessy in the middle of a blizzard."

Had he asked her directly if Hennessy was in fact Michael Watkins, she could not have felt more uncomfortable. She told as much of the truth as she could muster. "I had reason to believe he knew I was onto him." She drew her knees up and locked her arms around them. "That he would split. Make a run for it." She looked directly into Jack's eyes. "We keep bumping up against the truth here, Jack."

"Which is?"

"Which is that you don't want to know who or why or how I knew what I knew. Or what the stakes were. Why I chose to go after him up there, alone and in a blizzard, has a certain history behind it."

He turned and poked at the poorly burning logs. A spray of sparks like firecrackers shot up the flue. Heat began to emanate into the room.

Still he watched the fire. "We never talked much about what went on in your life, with your father. I got the gist of your life history the afternoon I saw you in that intersquad volleyball game. The consensus was it's being Louis Difalco's little girl that makes you tick. Honor. Duty. Justice. Nightmares.''

She swallowed. "Why do people do that? Presume to know what makes anyone do what they do?''

"It's human nature, Becky.''

"So common wisdom would hold that only the specter of the Bushwhacker could make Louis Difalco's otherwise intelligent daughter desperate enough or determined enough to scrap the rules and tramp up that mountainside after a known murderer—without backup.''

"That would about cover it.''

"It would be wrong.''

"I'm not so sure, Becky.'' He met her eyes. "It is Michael Watkins you're after, isn't it?''

"Yes. It is. But not because I have to redeem my father's misspent life, Jack.''

"You believe Hennessy is Watkins?''

In that instant she knew the source of all her anxiety. She scraped her hair again. "Yes.''

He swore softly. The firelight flickered over his hardened expression. "Is he pulling off another extortion attempt?''

"I believe he is. I don't know what he wants, but—'' She broke off, staring at Jack, unsettled to her soul that he believed her when Aguilar and half a dozen others had not. "He made very sure I would find him in Rampart, Jack.''

He flicked the butt of his cigar into the stove. "Why you, Becky?"

"I don't know. At least, I didn't know until—" She broke off, searching her memory. Time had run together, and she couldn't remember how much time had passed since her discovery. "This morning, it was, sometime just past midnight when it hit me that it's been exactly twenty-five years since Watkins slipped away for good. From my father, to be specific. It's an anniversary of sorts, complete with Louis Difalco's daughter.

"Anyway." She shrugged. "I think he must have been planning the AirLife escape for a long time. He could set his destruction in motion and get away by hijacking the chopper, and I'd be left just like my father, a day late and a dollar short, so to speak."

"If that's all true, Becky, why didn't you go after him instead of coming with me?"

"I've been through every possible scenario in my mind, Jack. All the information we have, all the logic, the explosion, *everything* suggests there is no way Watkins survived a shoot-out with Sam Rosenberg and an explosion."

"Then—"

She held up a hand. "Wait. Let me get this out. I was thinking as we were driving up here—when you asked, in fact—that without his computer and satellite dish, even he couldn't pull off a remote terrorist attack. Watkins *must* have triggered the explosion, but I can't see it, Jack. I can't see him deliberately destroying his means of carrying through whatever terrorist act he planned to perpetrate.''

Jack shook his head slowly. ''Not unless he had some backup plan. But that doesn't answer my question. Why didn't you go up there and make sure Watkins was dead?''

His question finally set loose inside her the reason she had felt so anxiety-ridden over getting Jack to take her along on this rescue. ''It's because, even though all the logic and evidence suggest that Watkins was either killed by Rosenberg, hurt or escaped, I don't buy it.

''This is *the* Michael Watkins, Jack. This is a man who has every angle cold, and whatever adjustments he has to make are just...'' She searched for the right word to convey her sense of Watkins's native criminal brilliance. ''Inspired.''

''So tell me what you think happened, then.''

''I'm saying I think Rosenberg was worried that something happened to me. That he went up Rabbit Foot Hill to check it out, and that Watkins took Rosenberg's appearance for inspiration from the gods. I think the blizzard was about to ruin everything for him, so he improvised and murdered Sam. Then he called in an officer down, knowing that was the surest way to get the chopper launched, which he still intended to hijack.''

''So.'' He sighed heavily and shook his head, jamming another couple of logs into the stove.

"You knew, or suspected, that it was Michael Watkins we were going after all along."

The room felt suddenly too small to contain Jack's condemnation of her. His feelings about what she knew or didn't know or when she realized she would never believe it wasn't Watkins who had escaped on that AirLife launch hung heavily in the air.

"I didn't consciously know what I believed until just now, talking this through. Maybe I should have. Maybe I suspected it all along." Her chin went up. She knew her answer reeked of defensiveness, but it was the only one she had. "It wouldn't have made a difference, Jack. There are innocent crew members on that chopper. Even you would not have refused to go after them."

He began unlacing his boots, then jerked open the ties on his bedroll. With no hesitation, no false modesty, he pulled his sweater over his head, followed in short order by the white long underwear top beneath it. She turned away as if he'd asked her to, which he hadn't, which didn't save whatever delicate sensibilities she had left, anyway.

Over the snapping and popping of the flames in the stove, she heard what he was about and saw the faithful shadow he cast against the wall. Heard the clink of metal, saw him unbuckle his belt, untie the cover-ups, work loose his button jeans, kick off his boots and then his jeans. There wasn't a moment in all of that when her respiration ceased, but she felt exactly that sensation, the way she'd had the air knocked out of her when she fell scrambling down Rabbit Foot Hill.

He looked at her, standing in his long johns, idly rubbing his hair-matted chest with his shirt. "I hope you get what you want, Becky, because no matter what you believe, the only life worth living is the one you give up trying to set the world straight."

He slid inside the minus-forty-degrees, certified goose down sleeping bag and stuffed the wadded-up sweater and T-shirt under his head for a pillow. "Better pack it in. Get some sleep. We'll start at the crack of dawn."

But he lay there with his bare chest barely covered, arms out, gooseflesh spreading over his pecs and arms, beading his nipples while he went on dragging appreciatively at the cigar.

She didn't move for the longest time. After a while she knelt to toss a few more split logs into the stove, then went outside to relieve her aching bladder. But what she was really doing, she knew, was running from a half-naked, impossibly immodest, supremely easy-in-his-skin Jack Slade.

The one who made it his practice to live now and live hard, because nothing he could do in his life was ever going to set to rights the lives of the families of the children he hadn't been able to save.

And now, because of her, unless Michael Watkins had been killed in the crash, Jack was again involved in a potential disaster over which he had no more control than she.

ON HIS cross-country skis the following morning, Gunnar Schmit stopped at the headquarters of Rampart Mountain Rescue, in Jack Slade's building. The door was open. He let himself in and followed his nose to the back room. Jack's office.

Gunnar loved Jack's office. The pictures, the guys, the flight manuals, the maps. Sometimes when he hurtled down the mountain on his skis, he imagined what it must be like to be flying in a real whirlybird, especially in the mountains. Jack had offered to take him up, take him up, sure nuf, but Gunnar said no. He wanted to, wanted to bad, but he said no. Gunnar wouldn't trust himself not to wet his pants or throw up.

He had enough on his plate. Didn't need that, nope. Didn't need to make a fool out of himself. He had his dignity. But he drooled over the pictures in Jack's office, the cigar smoke. The whole place made Gunnar feel like one of the guys when he was there. One of the regular guys.

He stood inside the door, hands on his hips, staring at a picture of Jack grinning behind his aviator glasses, wearing his whirlybird helmet with the radio ears inside.

Gunnar had told Jack he ought to get a name on his helmet, like Maverick, but that was when he wasn't mad. But right now, right now Gunnar was pissed because Jack tried to pawn off a lie on him. Mick wasn't dead. But Jack was scout's-honor honest, so something was wrong.

A lot was wrong. The girl was bad news. Jack said he'd take care of it, but Gunnar didn't believe him. He was taking the girl's side.

"Gunnar, what the dickens are you doin' here?"

Zeb's cranky, tired voice put Gunnar over the edge, as if he were stupid or something. Like he didn't know enough to come in out of the rain.

He gnashed his teeth together so hard it hurt. "Thought I could help Jack. Help Jack, you know."

"Well, you can't. He's long gone. You oughta get yourself on home, stick by the fire and watch out you crack a window so the fire don't eat all the oxygen and starve your poor head any more."

"Always crack a window," Gunnar repeated like it was a rule. He knew that. Didn't he know that? "I know that, Zeb Tucker. Like I know you brush your stupid teeth. Like I know you better not cry and you better not pout." He was mocking Zeb— as if all he knew in the whole wide world was kid stuff.

He knew other things. He knew Mick didn't ever shoot at anybody with a sawed-off shotgun. That would be stupid. Gunnar hated to be lied to. He hated that worse than anything.

He had his dignity. People oughtn't lie to simple people like him. Simpletons like him had a b.s. detector like nobody else.

And Gunnar could keep a secret. He could even make up a secret if he wanted to, and cranky old Zeb would be the dummy.

"Hello?" Zeb intoned, making like that jerk knocking on Marty McFly's dad's head in *Back to the Future*. "Get yourself on home, now, Gunnar." This Zeb said more nice-like, but Gunnar stood firm.

"Where'd he go?"

"Jack?"

"Jack."

Zeb heaved a big sigh. "Gunnar—"

"I just wanna see on a map. I just wanna know where. Jack alwus shows me where he's goin'. Jack always shows me."

"If I do, will you go on home?"

Gunnar thought, yep, he's gonna tell me. But he didn't want Zeb sending Randy or coming around checking on him. "Nah. Gotta go shovel out a few places. I promised."

"You do that, Gunnar. Now come here and I'll show you on the topo where Jack went."

Gunnar sidled to the map. People always thought he was dumber'n a post when he walked like that. He didn't usually mind, cuz he got away with crap nobody else'd ever get away with.

Like now.

Zeb stabbed a finger at the yellow pushpin. "There. Right off the north face of this peak. Satisfied?"

Gunnar nodded dumbly. "How high?"

"Somewheres between eight and thirteen thousand feet."

Still nodding, Gunnar turned and shuffled toward

the door. "See ya round, Zeb." He didn't consider that he had lied. He felt no rumblings in his heart that he had betrayed himself by lying like a rug, like most people did. He would see Zeb around, only it just wouldn't be for a few days. He had to stop the girl. He had to do it now. If she thought Mick was the bad man she'd come looking for, she was plumb wrong.

"See ya round."

Chapter Six

Long before the sun came up, by the beam of a powerful flashlight, Jack unloaded the snowmobile, then hopped into the trailer to shove the rescue travois out. At the other end, Becky helped him tilt the sled past the wheel well, then straightened it so it slipped off.

The cold bit at her nose, paralyzed her lungs, cramped her legs. She took to the physical preparations with an almost manic energy. The only way she was ever going to make it was to warm herself from the inside out.

The depth of snowfall muted every noise save their labored breathing. Jack unloaded the snowmobile onto a three-foot cushion of drift. Anything but the most essential talking they avoided. Every calorie counted, every dram of energy, and wasting breath on idle chitchat just didn't happen.

He motioned for her to climb up and pass their gear to him. She traded places with Jack in the dark, shoving the supplies from the front of the trailer to the back. The small two-man tent, their cross-country skis. He loaded it efficiently on the sled, packing and repacking the gear, making his choices so the load would stay centered no matter what tortured, tilting, wild path the sled took behind the snowmobile, and later behind Jack as he skied or tramped through the mountains ahead of it.

"Anything else?"

She took the flashlight off the top of the Explorer and shone it around the trailer bed. "That's it." She handed him the flashlight, then took the gloved hand he offered her and jumped off the trailer.

He waved her to the side of the sled opposite him, then spread a waterproof tarpaulin over the gear. She took her side and followed his lead in tightly securing the cover. Her frozen, stiff fingers stumbled so much he had to come around and do the front end of her side himself.

"Sorry," she muttered, thinking he couldn't hear her over the howl of the fierce wind, keenly aware of two things—the pain in her shoulder, and the fact that they had yet to launch and already she had fallen behind.

"Do me a favor, Becky. Stow the apologies." His voice carried well enough beneath the wind. He wore a dark cashmere knit scarf around his neck and a bandanna pulled over his nose like a cowpuncher, concealing the puffs of his breath. "I'm not going to rub your nose in every damn shortfall from here to the crash site."

Yesterday she'd have snapped at the implication that there would follow a string of shortfalls on her part. Now, in the dark bitter cold and swirling snow, with her clumsy, gloved, frozen fingers already failing her, she spared herself the effort.

He rose off his haunches and gave her shoulder a squeeze as he went by her toward the snowmobile. Her throat thickened. Touching her, reassuring her was a kindness she might have expected but hadn't. She gave her tie-down a fierce pull to secure the knot, then turned and followed him.

She began kicking the drift in front of the machine while Jack disconnected the battery-operated engine-block warmer, then started the engine. When it caught and fired, the sound rumbled through the air.

She got out of his way and went to shove the front of the sled to an easier approach angle. He maneuvered the snowmobile into position and hitched the sled, then threw a leg over the seat. Becky climbed on behind him and put her arms around his waist.

"Ready?" he murmured over the low thrum of the idling engine.

She nodded, instinctively relaxing her body against his broad back.

He signaled his approval then throttled up and set the machine into forward motion, picking his way through the dark, towering age-old evergreens.

The quality of light changed, subtly opening up, making deeper shadows of the trees in the distance.

But the wind hurtled the snow around with such force he couldn't possibly have seen more than eight or ten feet in advance of the snowmobile.

They arrived at the crest of the hill above the cabin, maybe half a mile from the trailhead. Here the timberline gave way to a bald, treeless incline. Out of the protection of the trees, the wind howled off the higher mountains. Becky grabbed her goggles and pulled them up from around her neck to cover her eyes. The day grew lighter.

Jack slowed the machine so the sled eased over the incline from the uphill side to the downhill, then took the snowmobile into the protection of the timber line, angling sharply to the right. She looked for the reason, then saw a cove more or less protected from the wind.

Idling the engine, he reached into his pocket for the cell-phone-size Global Positioning System unit. She guessed he had plotted their jump-off position.

Turning so she could see what he was doing, Jack stripped off one glove and keyed in a few commands. The tiny screen glowed in the dark, the numerals indicating degrees of longitude and latitude in a bright, neon green against the darker background.

"This is where we are. Do you remember what key combinations get you our coordinates?" Talking over his shoulder, so near to her ear, he didn't have to shout over the wind or idling engine.

"Yes." She repeated the menu sequence.

"Great. This—" he punched another set of co-ordinates, taking the time to state what he had done "—is our destination."

She nodded. "Got it."

"What now?"

She knew how it worked, only the menu commands of this particular GPS were new to her. "Check our heading, compare to the direction of our intermediate targets and follow those vectors as closely as we can by the compass." There was no way to get from where they were now to where the chopper had gone down as the crow flies.

To navigate the physical barriers and impossibly steep, rocky slopes, they had to follow what looked on the tiny screen to be a jagged, meandering line connecting dots of a constellation of stars in the night sky.

He pointed out the compass on the dash of the snowmobile and read their bearing off the GPS unit. "You could do this on your own if you had to?"

"It might take me a minute or two longer, but yes, I think so."

He nodded, put the unit into a suspended state, pocketed it and headed out again. Over the course of seven or eight miles, the distance required to skirt a granite outcropping roughly the size of a cruise ship, they made fairly decent time. By nine o'clock they had reached the first of six intermediate destinations to the crash site. By noon, pushing hard in the mind-numbing subzero temperatures, they had reached the second, nearly a third of the way.

Jack eased off, stopping in the shelter of a clutch of protective evergreen, and killed the engine.

Becky stood, using Jack's shoulder to steady herself, and climbed off. The ground they had covered certainly justified the snowmobile, but in these whiteout, frigid conditions, her thigh muscles had stiffened unbearably. Her knees trembled, and her ankles, so long in one position, flooded with an excruciating pain.

Jack took one look at her fighting for balance, swung off the snowmobile and knelt in front of her. He planted his hands at her hips. "Steady. Just stand there a minute and let your circulation return."

A powerful shiver racked her torso. She gritted her teeth. "I'll be okay. You c-c-can let go."

"Yeah, in another couple of minutes."

He leaned into her so his shoulder supported her hips, then began running his hands hard up and down her legs, front and back, stimulating the blood flow to her extremities. She stifled a cry or two over the stinging pains of her flesh reviving.

She wore four layers of clothing—panties and silk long underwear beneath woolens beneath high-tech cover-ups. There was nothing even remotely sexual in his ministrations. He would have done exactly the same thing for a child or an old man or another woman. It meant nothing more or less than rubbing her own hands together.

But a moment came between needing more and needing less or no more of his attentions at all, the instant of lag when all her sensation had returned and she knew it.

"Jack."

His hands came to rest in a place on the backs of her legs beneath her bottom.

It was all so innocent. Therapeutic. Necessary, until their eyes met and deep inside her body desire, needfulness unfurled. She took a distracted step back. His hands fell away. "I'll be okay now."

He pulled down the scarf protecting his nose and mouth. "You're sure?"

"Yes." She felt suddenly, wildly irritable. His touch, his hands on her for any reason, most of all the underpinning of his concern for her, had undone her.

He could have looked away, let her off the hook in fairness for the number of times she had already done so for him, but he didn't. Instead he stood, closer than she wanted, closer than she could bear.

Fairness didn't hold sway in Jack Slade's world, only the here and now he refused to deny. He said nothing, but he didn't have to. The attraction between them flared from ember to flame, and she knew it as well as she knew anything.

She swallowed and pulled off her mask and shook out her short curls. She knew her irritation was irrational. What scared the hell out of her was that there was no way to combat what arose, what unintentional longing surfaced, what unwitting intimacy sprang from the unguarded moment.

"This can't happen, Jack."

He brought his hand to the side of her neck, his thumb to her chin. The blizzard, for all its intensity, might as well have died, for all she knew.

"You know what I've learned since I've been gone?"

"As little as possible?" she challenged.

"Not exactly."

"What then?"

His cold-roughened fingers stroked her neck. His thumb caressed her lips. His breath mingled with hers, heat and moisture colliding, coalescing, coming together as one in the bitter cold air and the pelting snow. She stood transfixed.

His head bent to hers. His black whiskers stood out starkly against his reddened cheeks. She turned her face aside, dipping her head, confused, wanting clarification, wanting to know what he meant to do. If he intended to breach the understanding she thought they had reached, to go beyond the accidental intimacy. And whether she would acquiesce and plunge into the breach herself.

He touched his stubbled cheek to hers, nuzzling her face. The contrast of soft and stabbing, the promise of a reckoning, the scent of danger made her go fiery deep into the pit of her body, and the quelling insistence for information died far short of words.

His lips brushed the angle of her jaw, the lobe of her ear, the curve of first one cheek, then the other, and at last her mouth. She closed her eyes, and in that other universe of chilled flesh and heated desire, she fell headlong into the avalanche of feelings.

She understood, suddenly, that she wanted to experience the randomness and joy of simple, uncomplicated abandon.

To let herself surrender, once, to elemental pleasure.

He groaned and pressed his body to hers. She sighed, struggled toward him till the disparity between the relentless, breathtaking cold and the feverishness between them compelled her to pull away, obliged her to make a joke.

"Is that what you've learned since you went away?"

"No." He drew back, exhaling harshly before she could learn what she would do if he offered her more, his eyes searching the sky, then a point beyond her shoulder, finally her own eyes. "What I've learned, Becky, is that things that can't happen, things that aren't supposed to happen, happen all the time."

He backed away from her, then turned and trekked into the trees. *Things that aren't supposed to happen, happen all the time.*

For a moment, she couldn't breathe. She could think of no argument, no answer, even if he had stood there waiting for one.

She knew the truth of it intimately, firsthand. And she knew from long and trying experience that when those things happened, you picked yourself up, dusted yourself off, pulled up your socks and went on, even if you were only five years old. Otherwise, excuses sprouted like weeds and you only wound up betraying yourself.

He could afford to let what happened happen.

She didn't have it in her.

She didn't for a solitary moment believe what intimacy sprang up between them would last beyond tomorrow or the next day or the day after that.

Between the two of them, nothing was simple, but one thing was sure.

Slade was coming nowhere near her heart.

She would remove herself from the possibility. She had only to take care of herself. If he thought he was going to have to baby her along, she would show him otherwise. All she had ever wanted was someone to watch over her, and to watch over in return. Jack could pull it off in conditions like these, doing whatever he thought it took to keep her fit enough to be of any use to him.

But all he really wanted ever after was the absolute freedom to neglect watching out for himself.

Pulling tissues from her coat pocket, she headed in the opposite direction through knee-deep drifts to make her own pit stop.

When she came back, he had already checked their heading and started the engine. The time was twelve-twenty. The blizzard was worsening, and they had hours to go.

THE DENVER METRO AREA went on an accident alert at three o'clock in the morning. Buttering a couple of slices of toast, Joe Aguilar had the radio on and heard the news. The highways were iced over, and the snow piling on top only made the conditions more treacherous.

He couldn't sleep. He had a prescription for sleeping pills, but he regarded people who medicated every little thing right out of existence as weaklings incapable of enduring life. That's what life was. An endurance test. And his sleeplessness had a specific cause that drugging himself would not alleviate.

His e-mail message to Becky Difalco had aborted. He couldn't be sure what portion of it went through or if she had gotten it at all.

From the moment his computer screen had flashed the abort message nearly thirty-six hours ago, he had been worried. He waited all day to hear from the feds. As of 1602 yesterday afternoon, he still didn't know if they'd had any better luck getting the necessary information to their agent or, if they had, whether Rosenberg and Becky had connected.

He finished his toast, wiped the crumbs and showered. By five o'clock he was dressed. He kissed his sleeping wife, checked on his teenage twin sons, left the house and backed down the hill at his Genessee home to the as yet unplowed road leading to I-70.

The foothills west of Denver usually got the heaviest snowfall. From what he could tell, this blizzard was no exception.

He shifted into four-wheel drive, turned from the access road onto the interstate ramp and began the slow trek down the mountain.

By noon yesterday, he'd assumed Becky had followed his orders and stayed away from the man she believed to be Michael Watkins. He didn't much care for assumptions, either, for the same reason he disliked medicating himself into oblivion. He wasn't available, either way, to deal with what came down the pike next.

With assumptions, you just hoped what you thought was true. You acted on incomplete information or not at all. You squandered precious time.

He dealt in facts and instinct. Over his years in law enforcement, he had honed to a razor edge his feel for what cops called a "situation."

Becky Difalco in Rampart, hot on the trail of one of the most heinous wanted criminals in the nation's history, was a situation.

He had the highest regard for her abilities, even in such circumstances as these. He had a good deal less faith that she would follow his orders.

He understood. When you were committed to risking your life for a greater good, the hardest thing in the world was obeying the order to stand down. He'd been there countless times in Vietnam. But on the face of it, even the likes of Michael Watkins stood at the mercy of a high-country blizzard that threatened to break all records.

He skirted a vehicle going down the mountain at no more than fifteen miles an hour and moved into the last lane, thinking that, yes, any assumptions he might have made about what Becky would do weren't worth a tinker's damn. At 1603 yesterday afternoon, he'd received a phone call from the feds.

According to some old man connected with Rampart Mountain Rescue, Sam Rosenberg had been evacuated from the scene of an explosion by an AirLife chopper that crashed within moments of lifting off Rabbit Foot Hill.

Aguilar tried for several hours to get hold of Jack Slade. He seemed to recall Rampart Mountain Rescue operated out of a building Slade owned. The phones were still out and would be for a while, so Aguilar had himself patched through by radio, only to find Slade was out on some rescue. If he understood the kid on the radio at Rampart, a woman matching Becky's description had accompanied Slade.

So Aguilar had been left with another set of assumptions based on skeletal information. The consensus of his staff held that he had nothing to worry about. He ticked off the reasons.

One, Rosenberg had been airlifted out. The probability stood at near one hundred percent he would not have survived the crash of the AirLife chopper. Nevertheless, he had been there to back up Difalco.

Two, Difalco had to have emerged from whatever fray took out Rosenberg if she had gone out on a rescue with Slade.

Three. If Rampart knew what happened to Rosenberg, even knew who he was, it had to have been Difalco who told them.

Four…and five. Aguilar had stopped listening, drawing the last unsubstantiated conclusion. An explosion on his property suggested that, in the best of all possible worlds, the Bushwhacker had met his demise in a manner befitting his crimes.

The available information wrapped this interpretation of the known events like a spiffy Christmas package.

Felice Navidad.

Aguilar's finely honed sense of a situation was that this package deal was a ticking bomb. He walked into his office, where all hell was breaking loose among the graveyard crew.

The switchboard operator couldn't manage a coherent sentence. Cussing the state system that saddled him with incompetent help, Aguilar ordered her to send the shift commander to his office.

He needn't have bothered. Sorenson was on the phone in Aguilar's office, shouting orders to get the forensic computer geeks on deck, posthaste. Either that or heads were going to roll.

Aguilar stripped off his coat and tossed it on the sofa. "What's going on?"

Sorenson dragged a hand through his thin, already-standing-on-end hair and swore. "The computer switching on the rail tracks paralleling Sante Fe Drive at Hampden just derailed a whole goddamn train. Parts of it are going up like a Roman candle."

Aguilar's first thought was of sabotage. "Have they determined the cause? How do they know the computer switching was responsible?"

"They don't, exactly."

"Then what the hell—"

Sorenson gulped. "The only thing they can get to come up on their system monitors is what looks like a photographic image of a tombstone."

A nasty taste arose in Aguilar's mouth. He bellowed at the rest of the available agents to get their butts into his office, then snapped at Sorenson. "Get them to screen-print the image and fax it to us."

Sorenson took a deep breath. Not one of the agents standing around in their cubicles made a move to gather as he'd ordered. "Am I in the twilight zone here? People?" he demanded.

Sorenson answered for them all. "No need of a fax, sir. The same image has frozen every computer on the CBI command network."

Aguilar swore. The foul taste in his mouth fragmented his attention. "How long?" he demanded, by sheer force of will keeping his sweetly buttered toast down.

One of the younger agents answered. "We can't tell for sure. The network was down for a routine archival download till an hour ago. When the system came online, this image came up. The best resolution we've got is on the twenty-five-inch monitor. Sir.''

He moved through the patch of four-foot-high cubicles in a fog, destined, he understood, for certain damnation.

The gravestone image, a low arch carved of granite, almost imperceptibly askew, sat in the foreground of a hundred others. Crosses, monuments, simple headstones, a mishmash of memorial stones in a Denver cemetery he recognized because his mother, Clarissa, was buried there.

He heard the young agent as if from a distance explaining that the computer was frozen. That the enhancement software could not be pulled up. That even with the aid of a magnifying glass Sorenson had received as a joke on his twentieth anniversary in the CBI, no one could quite read the name of the deceased, or the dates, for that matter.

But Aguilar could. Not that his vision was any sharper than that of the young bucks standing around the monitor, but because he already knew what it said. When you already knew, the letters reveal themselves as if by magic, clear as the signature of stars in the night sky.

He suffered a twinge of the minor angina he refused to medicate on principle. Heart pain, he had always maintained, was meant to give necessary warning. A wake-up call so you knew when to back off. Only he couldn't back off this one. Couldn't take it easy. Couldn't take a week off and sit in his rowboat trolling the lake for wily old trout.

He collapsed on one knee. He couldn't breathe. His mind went to an old country western tune and lyrics so inane, so out of the blue that he snorted. *Ya picked a fine time to leave me, Lucille...*

He knew his mouth gaped open and shut like one of those wily trout landed in his boat. With fish, you just banged their heads to knock them out. Put them out of their misery. But he wasn't a fish and he had a job to do and he refused to die first.

He had to get the name on that tombstone out or die trying, because all hell was about to bust loose on his watch because he had discounted the instincts of an agent in his own goddamned command.

Rule number one, Aggie, he told himself. Never discount the instincts of a subordinate you bleeding well trained yourself.

He gasped his last conscious breath. "Maeve," Aguilar croaked, collapsing with the effort to the floor.

"Maeve...Hennessy."

Chapter Seven

By their fifth hour out, they had reached the last navigable point on their course. With perhaps only a couple hours of daylight left to them, Jack figured they would leave the snowmobile and begin the descent to the crash site on foot.

The depth of snowpack, with the few feet of new snowfall, made it possible to take the snowmobile several miles beyond where he had expected to switch to cross-country skis. But it had also necessitated several minor adjustments to their course.

He had blanked everything else from his mind. These were the least grueling hours of all, considering the machine was doing all the work. He concentrated on the snowpack, the terrain, the landmarks, his compass bearings, the weather. The course charted on the GPS had given them the greatest gain in distance for the least possible trouble. Had their course adjustments been any more severe, making camp by nightfall would have been impossible.

He had schooled his mind against the intrusion of anything but coping with obstacles, circling back, choosing again, the constant challenge.

Which was why, he thought, guiding the snow-mobile toward the last stretch of navigable terrain, he had headed for the high country in the first place. A man could lose himself in the quest for survival, feed his hungry gut, fall into whatever passed for a bed and never think twice.

Save for the lack of his helicopter, he would have done nicely transported to the Stone Age. Survival left no quarter to higher ambitions or noble goals or the obligations of citizenship in a free society. He had walked away from all that and expected never to return.

The blizzard, the hijacking, the crash, the lives of innocent people at stake placed him squarely in the game.

Above them, the stark granite mountain peak rose to a height of more than fourteen thousand feet. Below them lay a vast geographic bowl, most of which was surrounded by sheer cliffs of heights from several hundred feet to as little as twenty-five feet. Taking the bowl around the uppermost ridge had put them in a position to avoid hauling themselves and the rescue sled up a seventy-five-degree incline to the crash site.

As the crow flies, Rampart was at most seven miles directly west of their position. He regretted the hours it had taken to skirt what would have been unnavigable by snowmobile towing the sled. But even on his own, he'd have had to make the same trade in hours to bring along even the barest provisions for a rescue.

He could feel Becky straightening behind him, stretching or searching, maybe, for any signs of the crash site in the expanse of mountainous terrain below them. Then he heard her low expression of dismay.

He slowed, brought the snowmobile to a halt and cut the engine.

"What is it?"

She put a gloved hand on his shoulder and dismounted, glancing uphill for a moment, then turning to look to a point about midway down the mountain. Pointing, she asked, "Isn't that about where we're expecting to find the crash site?"

He followed her direction. Snow swirled in near-blinding masses, but it was just possible, knowing where to look, to make out the landmark they sought, the outcropping of granite that had been graphically represented on the computer.

He raised his goggles to his forehead and peered through the flat light and flurries of snow, picking out the naked granite ledge. He saw no trace of the downed AirLife helicopter, but the ledge masked a shallow ravine, perhaps twenty feet deep. This was the site pinpointed by the triangulation on the emergency beacon. There they would find the chopper, concealed, trapped in the unforgiving gullet of stone and ice. "That's it."

Becky raked off her woolen hat and slapped at the crusted-on snow. "That's what I thought." She took a deep breath. "As far as we know, the crash site is within a couple of hundred yards of the ledge, right?"

"That's our fix, yes. What's wrong?"

"We've got a big problem, Jack."

"What do you mean?"

"We're going to have to be incredibly careful." She stuck her nose in her mitten for a moment, trying, Jack thought, to warm the air before the bitter cold assaulted her lungs. "See for yourself. Above the ledge."

Frowning, impatient, he turned and studied the ledge and all the terrain above it. The higher up the mountain he looked, the more impossible it became to distinguish geologic features, the snowfall from the crust, the flurries from the drifts. "I don't see—"

"It's a cornice. Look about fifteen degrees clockwise from the ledge. You can just see the slightest glint of light where the snowdrift begins to curl over the top of itself."

He took a pair of binoculars from a compartment below the seat of the snowmobile. He got off the machine, stood beside her and focused the binoculars at the top of the ridge he'd intended to traverse.

Exactly where she'd indicated, he finally spotted

the enormous cornice of snow, like an ocean wave solidified and surging powerfully forward, rolling over on itself, creating a massive, deadly overhang of snow.

He swore softly. "That's one lovely piece of work." He lowered the binoculars. "You didn't happen to spot the chopper, too, did you?"

She rolled her eyes. She knew, he thought, that he was teasing her. "No," she answered. "I'm good, Jack, but not that good. It was just a trick of the light that I even saw the cornice."

"I don't want to think about what might have happened if we weren't paying attention to it." He pulled a canteen of water from beneath his coat, drank half of it, then offered the rest to her.

"Thanks."

"You're welcome."

"I don't see how we can avoid working beneath it, do you?"

He shrugged. "Can't be helped."

A violent shiver rattled her bones. Her chill gnawed at him worse than his own. He could barely keep his hands to himself, keep from giving her his coat.

"Do we have enough daylight left to get down and set up camp?"

"Yeah. We'll be cutting it close to get the sled down before dark, but we're going to have to dig out a snow cave first. I don't want to risk sleeping in a tent with that cornice hanging over us. Think you can handle it?''

''No sweat.'' But she made no move to get aboard the snowmobile. She drank from the canteen in small, steady swallows and looked in the distance at the potentially death-dealing overhang. ''Is there any chance that if the cornice breaks off, the weight of it would bury the chopper?''

He lifted the binoculars again, studying the contour and vertical drop. ''The terrain is much more likely to support a slide. But if the cornice does break off, it'll drop like a stone. Probably cut us off completely.''

''But the chopper won't get buried.'' She glanced rapidly away from him, her lips pulling down. She stared up the mountain, her eyelids batting furiously.

''Becky?''

''I just caught myself thinking an avalanche wouldn't be so bad,'' she confessed, sniffing and swiping at her reddened nose with the back of her mitten. ''For a moment there, I really didn't care if the AirLife crew makes it out alive or not, just so Watkins doesn't.'' She shoved her hood back and tore off her face mask. ''I'm not very proud of it, but there it is.''

He cocked his jaw. He knew all about ignoble feelings, what it was to want another human being to suffer and die in ways more unkind even than the suffering they had inflicted. Everybody had them.

He'd had them. In spades. Like survivors who

wanted some murdering bastard to die twice and in agony for every innocent life he took. The difference was, he'd felt all too prepared to exact the price himself.

You wound up wanting it more than you wanted to keep living yourself, more than you cared who else had to suffer. But in Jack's case, the bastard in question had turned his weapon on himself, so Jack was left with the rage and instinct to exact a fitting vengeance with nowhere to take it.

Becky may have made the conscious decision not to live her life as Michael Watkins's victim, but she had no clue, *wanted* no clue that she had nevertheless been emotionally maimed.

He thumped the brim of his hat to knock snow off it. He knew the dark underbelly of her soul like he knew his own. "It's pretty shocking to find murder in your own heart, isn't it?"

Her chin went up.

"You're not the only one who ever—"

"I'll tell you what it's like," she interrupted fiercely. "It's like I *am* the only one. I know I'm not the first person to feel like this. I won't be the last, either. But…" She shook her head. "I don't want to sink to Watkins's level, Jack. Not even in my thoughts."

"Get over it." He'd accepted his inhumanity. Embraced it and then abandoned it. He felt like a shit dealing with her so harshly, but they didn't have time to indulge her guilt or remorse or whatever the hell tender sensibility she was feeling.

She swallowed hard, but she wasn't one to stand there and take whatever flavor of abuse he doled out. "Do you ever get over it?"

"Does *one* ever get over it, you mean?"

"No. I mean do—"

"Maybe." He interrupted her attempt to clarify her question. "Will I?" He shook his head slowly. "Not a chance. Get over that, too, while you're at it, Becky. You're asking the wrong man."

"I don't think so."

"Think again."

She looked steadily at him, unflinching, sniffling, shivering like a drenched puppy, daubing at her nose, refusing to cave in to his coarse refusals.

He couldn't believe he was standing here in the middle of a blizzard—in this godforsaken terrain, in these temperatures and conditions, with the snow freezing to her eyelashes, brutalizing her skin and sapping all their energy—having this argument with her.

"I think I'm asking exactly the right man. I know what you've said about yourself. I know you walked away, and I know you have no intention of going back to who you were. What I'm asking is if you believe in your heart that you can get away with it for the rest of your life and still live with yourself."

His tongue was well and truly stuck, rooted to the pit of his mouth. Her doggedness made him want to lash out at her. Her question took sweet and deadly aim at his soul. He felt as if he had been sucker punched, as sick inside as if she had kneed him in the groin.

He wanted to return the favor. Hurt her. Take a stab at pointing out to her how clueless she was to believe that justice would finally out.

But as much as he wanted to punish her, he also wanted to take her in his arms, hold her, make the clash of worlds between them disappear to ease at least his own pain.

Maybe lie and assure her he really was the man she insisted he still was.

Or lie a little more and promise her he could be that man again if she stuck around long enough that he began to believe it again, in spite of himself.

Maybe go all the way with his lies, like a man goes all the way with a woman, letting her believe it was love and not lust. Somehow pretend. Somehow delude himself that he understood why the hell she cared enough to have it out with him in this blistering, unforgiving deep freeze.

The wind howled through the trees. A branch cracked cleanly off a winter-nuded tree. Brittle, frozen trunks creaked ominously.

And his eyes collided with hers.

He couldn't bloody breathe. He saw that frigging hero worship coming at him, that expectation of a better man tearing him up inside, and he hated her for it.

She had it down, all right, if it was true that you never hurt anyone more than you hurt the one you love. Or, in her misguided case, the one she thought she might have loved.

He didn't have it in him to measure up, and if he had to tell her one more time or fifty, fine. But it took everything in him to draw breath, to conjure a level, disinterested tone of voice.

"I can live with myself. That's the difference between us, Becky. We won't ever end up a matched set because you want to take on the world, and I just want it to go away and leave me the hell alone."

"You know what, Jack?" A tear fell to her cheek and froze in an indelicate chunk. "I think you love your story. I think—"

"Oh, that's rich."

"You do!" she accused. "You love your little drama. Isn't it bad enough, Jack? Yes! Children died. It's hideous. And you didn't stop it. But you know what, Jack? No one could have stopped that shooter. No one," she repeated. "But you think if you had been a better man, if you had been a man at all, you would have stopped it. Who do you think you are? What do you think you could have done? How many hours did you try talking the guy out of his frenzy? Sixteen? Seventeen?"

"Nineteen," he snarled. "Trust me. I was counting every second."

"Who could have done more?" she cried.

"Stop it, Becky. Just shut up and leave it alone."

"Don't tell me to leave it alone, Jack. I won't. How dare you tell me to get over it and stand there behaving like you're the one who's entitled to wallow in it!"

He clamped his mouth shut before he said something he knew he would regret. Then he turned away. "We're wasting precious daylight."

"You're wasting something far more precious than a few hours of daylight, Jack, and you know it."

"Yeah. I am." He swiped the snow from the seat, got on board and teased the engine to life. "But you always knew that, didn't you?"

HAMPERED BY ever deepening snow and the flat, meager light waning in the late afternoon, progress down the mountainside became torturous. She wanted time, needed the space to consider where their argument left them, what it meant.

Whether she believed he would ever get over the tragedy that had cut him off from the man he really was.

But no more than another hundred yards down the slope they came upon the granite landmark. Hanging out over a thirty-five-foot drop, the ledge was maybe fifteen feet wide at its middle, gradually giving way to no more than a couple of feet at either end. Jack spotted a narrow chute they could descend on foot, but after they had dug out a suitable snow cave, they would have to go up and belay the sled down.

There would be no time or distance away from Jack. No time to consider that the anger she felt and the anger she had provoked in him unmasked much deeper, far more intimate feelings between them.

Shivering, she stepped back from the emotional precipice to consider the physical one confronting them. There was no other way, she knew. Jack retrieved a couple of small collapsible shovels from the equipment piled beneath the tarp on the sled. She followed him as he backed down the narrow chute, kicking makeshift footholds into the snow.

At the base, as Jack had predicted, there was an enormous drift at least marginally suited to make a snow cave.

Jack stripped off his backpack and loosened his coat, then set to work. He hollowed out an entrance on a fairly steep upward angle, then began to level out at a height above the entrance of about two and half feet—the minimum to insure that the coldest air, being heaviest, would sink to the ground outside the cave.

Remaining outside the entrance, Becky shoveled to keep pace with Jack, clearing away what he scooped out. That done, he fashioned a sleeping platform another two and half feet above the floor of the cave, then they both worked to compact and smooth the ceiling of snow to minimize dripping.

The task took an hour and a half, but by the time he was done, they could both easily stand inside the igloo shape.

Getting the sled down the thirty-five-foot drop was going to eat up the remaining daylight. They made their way up the chute, and Becky helped Jack organize the ropes necessary to lower the loaded sled.

He chose a crack a few feet off dead center of the ledge and drove an anchoring piton into the granite. In the deepening darkness, it was going to be easier to belay themselves down than to risk the chute a third time.

He gave her the rope, which he would use to rappel down the side to attach to the bolt. She knew he wanted to watch her work, inspecting her belaying knots to satisfy himself she could secure any line.

After he was down it would be too late to discover deficiencies. He would use the same rigging to rappel himself, then lower the sled on belay and finally assist her belay.

Unhappy with her first effort, she started over. Her fingers were numb from the bitter cold. She had no idea how she made them perform to any acceptable standards. Somehow, she managed.

In the meantime, Jack stepped into his seat harness, pulled the loops at his groin tight and buckled the belt around his waist. He shoved the sled into position and worked with a couple of bungee cords to tighten the load.

He gave her one last measuring look. "This is it. You know the drill."

She nodded. "As soon as you're down, you'll signal. I'll reverse the rope and tie on the sled. You'll control the belay, I'll haul the rope up one last time, clip onto my harness and follow.''

He nodded and clipped on his harness carabiner. ''If you have any doubt about what you're doing at any point—''

''I'll ask. Now go. Let's get this puppy down.''

He threw the seventy-foot rope in an expert toss over the cliff so its weight cleanly unraveled the coil. In seconds he was over the edge, as well, out of her sight.

In her imagination she saw him hanging over the darkened abyss, saw him shoving off the wall, gliding down the rope, breaking his speed, belaying himself half the length of the rope. She counted only one muted thrust against the side before the tension went slack on the rope.

''Off rappel,'' he shouted, signaling his safe descent and that he had freed himself of the rappel rope. ''Take it up, nice and easy.''

Easy. In the profound silence, damped by an unimaginable weight of snow, the word echoed.

Once.

Twice. *Easy.*

The light subtly changed, one moment flat but very much a comforting presence, the next shadowed, darkened, lost. She felt a distinct chill. She had never been afraid of the dark in her life. In the dark was where she had been safe, where her life had been spared beneath the sofa in the house that collapsed around her.

But the sun setting on the blizzard before she could get down unnerved her. Working automatically to ward off tension, hand over hand she gathered in the rope and prepared to snap the carabiner at its end onto the sled bolt.

She stepped into her seat harness, listening to the eerie howl of wind, but stopped, frozen, when, in its wake, she heard a harsh whisperlike, gliding sound, like the scrape of skis over the wind-hardened shell of snow.

Her throat tightened. Fear coiled inside her. The sound was so extraordinary, so out of place in this frozen wilderness. She heard the rasp again. She knew of nothing the sound could be but skis.

She called out. "Hello? Is anyone out there? Hello?"

She glanced all around, saw nothing, heard nothing but the labored sound of her breathing. Her uneasiness grew. A frozen lump of irrational dread formed in her breast.

"Becky?" Jack called. "I'm right here."

Here…here.

Echoes, she thought, her dread easing. Only echoes. The rasping whisper had seemed to come from behind her, from deep in the towering monster trees, but maybe it had been Jack, scraping aside a drift of snow to anchor himself for the equipment belay.

Surely that was it, the echo of his efforts.

"On belay!"

She realized it was the third time he had called to indicate he was prepared to take down the sled. Her nose prickled. The time remaining to execute lowering the sled and her own belay over the precipice was nearly extinct.

"Jack? Jack, are you there?" *Are you ready?* That's what she'd meant to ask. Of course he was there. Of course he was ready.

"Becky. You've gotta move, babe. Now. Don't think. Just do what you've got to do," he called.

She recognized the tone of his voice, the calm, the urging, the kind of encouragement an adult reserves for a child terrified of pointing her skis downhill on what amounted to no more than a bunny slope.

You're safe, it said. *You'll be fine.*

She had asked for the reassurance by calling to him, but she resented it. She sat on the crust of frozen snow, her feet lodged in their boots against stone, her legs trembling. Her back ached. Her injured shoulder throbbing, her mind numbing in the cold, she knew the unreasoning fear of that rasping, whispering noise had robbed her remaining sensibilities, her dwindling energy stores.

But it isn't unreasoning, she thought. Maybe she was at the point of hypothermia, of her brain not working properly. But the uneasiness inside her had nothing to do with the bitter cold sapping her, nothing at all to do with her abilities or the energy she had left.

She commanded her sluggish muscles to follow his instructions quite mindlessly, if that was what it finally took.

Jack shouted again at her, encouraging, urgent. She could manage. Even in the black of night, she could manage if she had to. But she had never felt so alone, so utterly…isolated.

She breathed as deeply as she dared. Whatever threatened, real or imagined, all she could do was get off the ledge.

She began to follow his lead, to act, not think. She jerked the knot on her line tight. Taking the back sled line, she made her final preparations.

Her line would prevent a nasty drop on his end when the full weight of the sled went over the edge.

He called out one last time.

She knew all about his impatience. When you were wading in deep snow and horrendous cold, when daylight was gone and all you wanted to do was keep moving while your energy lasted, waiting for anyone was pure hell.

At times like this, seconds passed like minutes, minutes like hours, and it didn't matter whether you had teamed up to climb Everest or work a rescue.

Satisfied she could control the drop of the sled, she began chanting some mindless encouragement to herself, then planted her body firmly behind the anchoring piton. She released the first coil, then another and another until the sled, inching by its weight toward the edge, hung in the balance.

One more coil, she thought.

One more.

"On belay!" She braced again. Leaning back by degrees, she took the ropes in a counterclockwise motion with both hands, then fell back to counter the tremendous drop of dead weight created by the sled hanging suspended over the edge.

The anchoring piton held. Without thinking, she eased her body forward, letting out more rope until she heard Jack shouting, "Twenty feet...ten, five...we're almost there...it's down."

She struggled to her feet and began hauling in the rope. The light of day was gone. She worked as much by feel as by sight. Her eyelashes felt crusted with ice, her hands and fingers brittle and unworkable with cold.

Tugging with her meager remaining might to assure herself her rope would hold, she trudged toward the precipice, positioning herself to go backward over the edge and let Jack belay her to safety.

Only then, from out of the darkness, the whispered scraping noise came again, and this time from very nearby. Her throat constricted, and her labored breathing ceased. An enormous black figure loomed out of the darkness.

She shut her eyes and willed herself to take that backward step off the precipice, but a slicing noise whistled in the silence, followed by the appalling sensation of her tether slackening.

She heard herself scream. The knowledge that her rope had been cut only penetrated her brain after her body reacted, hurtling her forward rather than back, protecting her from a plunge.

Jack shouted to her. Dimly recognizing the alarm in his voice, she screamed for him, then fell heavily forward.

She understood what a serious mistake her natural instincts had caused in the split second before the enormous black figure towered over her. She screamed again and hurled herself at its knees, but a powerful hand clamped down on her hood and snapped her head back.

She writhed and fought, refusing to go easily, dimly certain only Watkins would come this far, go to such terrifying lengths to destroy her. She reached up and clamped her hands on his wrist and lifted herself by force of will, bringing her knees toward his groin, but he guessed her trick and dropped his arm, causing her to fall.

And then a heavy, gloved fist came at her and, though she ducked, knocked her cold.

Chapter Eight

"Becky! Becky, answer me! What's going on?"
Jack shouted. Backing up to get a line of sight to
the cliff edge, he listened for an answer. All he heard
was a deep grunt, deeper, he thought, than Becky's
voice. Then the rope he would have used to belay
her slunk surrealistically over the cliff, and the
sound of silence closed over a muted clump...
clump...clump.

The sound, he knew instantly, of boots thudding
against the heel plates of cross-country skis.

He ran toward the rope and picked up its end. He
pulled out his butane lighter and examined the rope,
seeing that it had been cleanly severed. He shouted
again and again, knowing all along at some primitive level that it was useless.

Becky wasn't going to answer.

She had been silenced, most likely dragged off.
Near the point of physical exhaustion, he could not
imagine a scenario in which what had happened
could happen.

The echo in his mind stung. *Things that can't happen, happened all the time.* But this went beyond the pale, beyond the wildest circumstance. They had to have been followed, pursued, and all Jack could think was that Michael Watkins was the only man alive who wanted Becky Difalco dead and wanted it bad enough to go to these lengths.

Jack swore violently.

Watkins was alive and had improvised brilliantly. She'd picked one piss poor time to be dead right. Watkins had not only survived, he'd known she would come after him, that she would believe, despite any and all evidence to the contrary, he had escaped on that medevac chopper.

Jack found another rope, a grappling hook and a couple of ascenders with loops attached. He knew Watkins had not planned this. He had meant to lure her to his lair, but not in the most godforsaken blizzard of the century and some of the most grueling territory on earth. Even Watkins could not have predicted with such accuracy Becky's arrival in Rampart, the timing of the storm or Rosenberg happening along to foul up his plans.

But what he lacked in luck, Watkins more than compensated for in sheer animal cunning.

It took him too many crucial seconds to prepare an ascent. He ripped loose the tie-downs on the tarp covering the sled and the bulk of his climbing equipment, then threw onto the loops on his pack a loop of pitons and a hammer, his ice ax and a couple lengths of rope.

His fatigue was no longer an issue. An outrage he'd once sworn he would never again entertain consumed him. It was true he had been made a fool of, that he had been bested.

That he had failed to note the pursuit of a madman.

That he had failed to watch his own back, never mind Becky's.

And that he deserved to suffer the consequences of his obscenely unwitting neglect.

He almost expected the comeuppance. He had, after all, turned his back on what he knew best, what he did best, which was to talk down the scum who held hostages and threatened innocent lives or, failing that, take them down.

No. He suddenly understood, hurling the grappling hook again and again until it caught and held, that it wasn't the living and dying by the sword that condemned him. It was the abandoning of the sword altogether.

Becky Difalco had not, and he swore on whatever the hell was left sacred in his life that she would not suffer the consequences he so richly deserved. But, to swear it at all, he had to imagine he would not find her dead.

He pulled his cross-country skis and poles from their position along the length of the sled, then bound them to the sides of his pack along with his rifle and scope.

Nothing could be more awkward, but he wasn't long on choices. He hung the radio and GPS units around his neck, then eased his arms into the shoulder straps, every effort clean and sparing. He tested the rope, then threaded it through the ascenders and began his climb.

He first shoved high up on the rope one ascender, connected to the carabiner at his waist, then the other, which supported the loops for his feet. The metal contraptions slid easily up the rope and clung tightly with the downward pressure of his weight. Quickly, but carefully, he began his ascent.

At the top, the cold and ice compromising his grip on the rope, he pulled himself over the edge, searching the landscape for the prone shape of a lifeless body. Of Becky's body.

He realized she wasn't there, wasn't lying dead anywhere nearby. A sick sort of relief flooded him, but it lasted about two seconds. He pulled a flashlight from a hero loop at his side and cast its cone of light in the darkness, seeing for himself her backward footprints over his own. He noted with a fierce determination how close she had come to lowering herself to safety and where she had fallen forward after the belay rope had been cut.

And how she must have struggled.

If only she had allowed herself to fall back, he'd have caught her on belay and Watkins would have been left stranded, at least for that crucial moment, on the ledge.

Becky would never quit. He knew that at best her refusal to give up had forced Watkins to knock her senseless. A sharp emotion for her, fierce and fiery and tender, grabbed at his throat.

Still he worked steadily, cleanly. A set of ski tracks led to the ledge from the deep woods, and back again cutting deeper to one side as her attacker Telemarked up the slope.

By the tracks, deeper on one side than the other, Jack knew Watkins was bearing her weight on his left shoulder.

He jerked loose the ties binding his skis and poles. He knew he had a better than even chance of overtaking them. He beat the snow off the soles of his boots and bound each in turn to a ski, then took off after them, following the tracks. His eyes adjusted to the dark and to the forbidding landscape about him. He easily tracked Watkins's progress through the snow.

He took a couple of seconds to try raising someone at Mountain Rescue. The radio hung from a leather strap around his neck. He pulled it from beneath his coat and pressed the send button. The glowing red light indicated that the battery was fully operational. He brought the unit close to his chapped and cracking lips.

"Rampart, this is Slade. Do you copy? Over." He gave it ten seconds, repeated, then another ten and one last try, but all he got was static. He hadn't expected different results, not the way things were going. But a change in plans this drastic called for advising the home base.

With the tips of his skis at a near forty-five-degree angle to each other, he started up the killing slope at a rapid clip, keeping his breathing even, his expenditure of oxygen at a minimum.

He had what little remained of his character on the line, and for a few moments all he could think was that the Reverend Jonah Slade, his father, would be cackling his ass off in secret. His errant, prodigal, prideful, smooth-talking son had turned from God and earned yet another encounter with forces beyond his control—the comeuppance of a man without the balls to sustain a little character in the face of affliction.

His father, of course, would have said the *fortitude* to sustain character. To consider the chance that his father had always been right, that a man with the integrity of a snake-oil salesman could have seen through Jack well enough to predict he would inevitably walk away from his responsibilities, felt like a gutting.

Living beneath his father's half-assed hallowed roof meant Jack answering to and for every infraction that came to the old man's attention. If Jack didn't do it, he'd caused it. If he hadn't caused it or even been there when something untoward occurred—when his sister ran away, for instance, or his younger brothers took a five-finger discount on whatever struck their fancy at the mall—then he should have been.

Either way, the blame fell to Jack. He had his father to thank for his gift of gab, his glib, gilded tongue, his finely honed aptitude for talking his way out of any peril.

It had served him well until he ran up against the maniac holding innocent kids and a plain-faced, eager young teacher hostage with an AK-47. Then he learned his genius had its limits.

That he couldn't prevail every time.

That he was little better than the fraud his father had been, promising miracles, delivering a good deal less.

After the carnage at the middle school, Jack stopped promising miracles. And that was the way he lived with himself.

Ask me no questions, I'll tell you no lies.

He stopped long enough to bend at the hips, to give his hamstrings a stretch, his lower back a respite, and to drive the image of the Right Reverend Slade from his mind.

He must have killed an hour reaching an abrupt downward shift in the terrain. Still, he followed through the pelting whiteout black-of-night blizzard without difficulty, and the ease of it began to gnaw at him. The exertion of skiing kept his energy up and his body heated, but he began to consider the possibility that he was moving into an ambush.

A trap.

There was no way to move through the snow without leaving a trail. Watkins knew that, of course, as well as he would have to know that Jack could move fast enough to catch up. Given the creep's incredible resourcefulness, Jack had to assume the worst, that Watkins was enough in the lead to dump Becky and lie in wait for him.

Anticipating Watkins's downhill pattern, Jack cut between the trees, closely following the vertical drop. Unencumbered, he could move through the trees, crouching and dodging, gaining valuable time.

But as he reached the edge of the trees where a wide swath of a glacier terminus cut through the landscape, he heard a motor rumble to life, an engine far larger than the one in the snowmobile.

Disbelief spread through him like a draft of hemlock. He broke out of the treeline and onto the glacier remains, grateful for the thickly layered snow, and aimed his skis downhill. Then he rounded the glacier's edge.

And what he saw made his blood run more cold than if it had been Michael Watkins.

GORDY KUBIAK FOLLOWED the ambulance conveying his boss to the county hospital, waited outside the ER where Aguilar's labs were pulled and an EKG was performed and where, in the course of eight hours, he went twice more into cardiac arrest.

There wasn't anyone on duty anywhere—not at

the FBI, not the CBI nor any of the near one hundred local police stations and sheriff's office in the metro area or the state—who recognized the name of May Hennessy.

Gordy had called in favors with a couple of local journalists, but neither had been able to dig up an answer. Part of the problem was that it was impossible to tell when the woman had died. If it was even twenty years ago, it might as well have been a thousand.

But clearly, Joe Aguilar had struggled hard to get the name out because he believed the identity would be meaningful. And just as certainly, the extent of his heart attack had to do with his reaction to the name. Gordy had no choice but to wait at Aguilar's bedside, hanging out with the hospital smells, drinking endless cups of coffee until Joe came around enough to say who May Hennessy was and why it mattered.

Twelve dicey, tedious hours passed before Aguilar regained consciousness. Gordy was right there.

Squinting, his boss started to reach for the bed rail to pull himself upright.

"Joe, you've got to stay still. We have to talk, but they'll boot me out if you get all hot and bothered."

Aguilar let his head fall back and gave an exhausted nod. "I want...I want you to get Louis...Difalco in here."

"Here? At the hospital?"

"Yes."

Gordy frowned. "Becky's old man?"

Aguilar gave a single nod.

"I don't understand. Joe, who is May Hennessy?"

Aguilar breathed deeply, preparing himself, then lifted the oxygen mask. "Maeve Hennessy was the daughter of a sitting justice of the Colorado Supreme Court and Michael Watkins's girlfriend."

"When did she die?"

"She was killed February sixth. Twenty-five years ago today."

Gordy sank to the chair beside the bed. "How did it happen?"

Aguilar lifted the oxygen mask from his nose and mouth. "Stray bullet."

Joseph Aguilar hung his hat on bedrock values, and as if a mind like a steel trap were not enough, he had a near-photographic memory, the instincts of a beat cop, the nose of a Mississippi bloodhound.

But Gordy Kubiak was no slouch himself, and he didn't need reading glasses to decipher the handwriting on the wall. "The gravestone image is Watkins's signature on the train wreck, then."

Aguilar managed a nod.

"One last hurrah in Maeve's memory. One final stab at the last word. What do you want to bet the photo is plastered all over the front page of tonight's paper?"

Grimacing, Aguilar clapped the oxygen mask

over his nose and mouth, took a few deep drafts and struggled to conclude. "Don't kid yourself. He's not done."

"Wait a minute." Maybe he needed the reading glasses after all. "Is Louis Difalco involved?"

"No. Becky is. She went to Rampart. She went after him."

"Rampart? After Watkins?" Gordy asked, incredulous. "By herself?"

"It's..." Aguilar gave a foreshortened, painful sigh. "Complicated."

"Joe, I'm sorry to be so dense, but I don't get it. If she needs backup we'll get on it. Do you want her old man apprised of the situation?"

"No." Pain etched itself in the crow's-feet about Aguilar's eyes and the rictus of his lips. It was clear to Gordy that Joe was enormously frustrated, that his thinking went far beyond what he had been able to verbalize. His vital signs began to go haywire, and the nurse moved quickly to send Gordy out and calm her patient. But Aguilar protested and clung to his hand.

"I want to know why," he gasped. "I want Louis Difalco to tell me why."

HER FIRST conscious thought was of the bruising pain to her abdomen. She had no thought or prayer that she was simply caught up in some unending nightmare. The bitter cold and dark, the dizzying swirl of snow, the wind howling through the trees were all too familiar.

The jolting pain each time she bounced against her captor's shoulder was not. Unable to draw a full breath, she could barely muster the energy to cry out.

"Put me down!"

He halted midstride, leaned to his left and let her fall heavily to the ground. Her injured shoulder took the brunt of her weight. She drew her first unimpeded breath and got to her knees.

She could not have been more vulnerable. He had only to cuff her upside the head to silence her. Or leave her where she fell to succumb to hypothermia in a matter of minutes.

Too numb to care what became of her for defying Watkins, she took several small breaths, peeled off her mask and glared at him. "You'll never get away with this."

"Never get away with this." He stood behind his mask looking at her and shrugged. "Don't matter none at all."

Shock roiled through her body, nausea or relief in its wake. "Gunnar?"

"Sure nuf it's Gunnar," he agreed, then scowled. "You shouldn'ta come to Rampart. Shouldn'ta come out here after Mick, neither."

It took her sluggish mind too many beats to get that it was not Watkins who had come after her but a simpleminded Gumpish man obsessed with one overriding objective—to prevent her from hurting or killing his friend.

Her only chance lay in convincing Gunnar she would not. He was unlikely to believe her, but she had to try. "Gunnar, please. Listen to me. I came out here with Jack. He needed me to assist with a rescue. There's an AirLife helicopter down—"

"You don't tell the truth. Jack shouldn'ta brought you. You only want to shoot Mick dead." He turned away to trudge on.

"Gunnar, wait!" She scrambled to her frozen feet, dismayed that in the midst of a felony in kidnapping her, Gunnar managed to ignore her protest and string together three complete and maddeningly irrational sentences. "Gunnar!"

He turned, saying nothing. Only ten feet away from her, he was little more than a shadowy figure in the thick, blowing snow. He didn't move a muscle, only appeared to stare blankly at her.

She looked where they had come from. Even deep in the forest the snow had all but covered the tracks of Gunnar's skis. She would never be able to follow them back, even if she could have found the physical stamina to accomplish on foot what Gunnar had done on skis.

"Listen." Her mind was working sluggishly. She desperately needed to stall him, to slow him down so Jack had a chance of catching up. Gunnar trusted Jack, at least. Or he had until he discovered Jack had taken her with him so she could murder his friend Mick.

But it was plain that her fate—if he left her here to freeze to death—wasn't anything that concerned Gunnar at all.

Who would ever know what Gunnar had done or that Gunnar was the one who had carted her off and left her to die?

She stamped her feet to drive her circulation and grabbed desperately for a subject to preoccupy him. "Gunnar, you know what? We don't even know if Mick was on the AirLife chopper. Even—"

"Mick was on the chopper," he repeated blankly. "Mick got away."

She stared uncomprehending at his hulking shape. "Gunnar, there was a terrible explosion up on Rabbit Foot Hill, at Mick's place. How do you know he got away? Did you see—"

"He got away," Gunnar repeated stubbornly, as if he knew for an absolute certainty that Mick was too clever to be trapped by the likes of her or killed in an explosion. "Mick is way smart."

"He is! Of course he is!" she cried, no longer able to keep even the barest check on her emotions. Gunnar was more right than he knew, more in touch with the fundamental truth on some terribly simplistic level than she had ever been.

Mick always got away.

Mick was way smart.

Add to that, she thought, Michael Watkins would

never be taken or stopped. Never die. But she couldn't cave in to her deepest fears, to her certainty that she could not win against Watkins. She would never say die. She had to keep trying to get Gunnar to turn back.

"Gunnar, if Mick is on that chopper, then he is probably hurt very badly. He needs help or he will never survive the crash, especially in this cold. Come with us," she implored.

But Gunnar wasn't interested in her reasoning. "Jack Slade will take care of it. You have to go now."

"How did you...how did you follow so closely? How are you going to get back?"

"Sno-Cat." He sounded petulant. Disdainful as any three-year-old explaining the patently obvious to his obviously uncool mother. "A Sno-Cat makes the snow safe and tight. A Sno-Cat goes up any mountain or down any mountain. It came here."

"Where is it?"

"Where is it. See, 'bout a half a mile more."

Her strategy in delaying Gunnar was working, but so was his. If she stood much longer, she wouldn't be able to move her feet at all, and then the end would come very quickly. She had no way of knowing whether Jack was coming after her or not, whether he could climb that treacherous thirty-five feet of cliff wall.

Even if he was coming, even supposing Jack Slade would find a way no matter what, her chances of surviving till then were looking very grim. A violent shiver took hold of her. Her teeth chattered mercilessly. She pulled her ski mask on. "Will you show me your Sno-Cat, Gunnar?"

"Not my Sno-Cat."

"Um…" Dear Lord. She wanted desperately to shriek at him that she knew the Sno-Cat wasn't his, but not so desperately as she needed to find a way, any way, to survive this, even if that meant humoring him. "I mean the one that came here? Will you take me there?"

He shrugged. "Take you there. Where else?" Again, the petulance.

"Good." Her jaw ached from her chattering teeth. "That would be really great." Shaking her hands to regenerate her upper body circulation, she went toward Gunnar. "Thank you for carrying me so far, Gunnar. But maybe I should just walk alongside you now. To keep my blood going."

"Keep blood going. Sure nuf."

He sounded almost friendly again. She tagged along beside him, fighting off her exhaustion, forcing herself to coach her body. *One foot in front of the other. Keep going. Just keep going.* After several minutes she asked if she was slowing him down too much.

"Too much," he agreed.

"Gunnar, are you still mad at me?"

"Still mad. You lied. Liars never prosper."

He began to ski a little faster, fast enough to make

her jog. If he was baiting her for a complaint, he wouldn't get one. "I thought that was cheaters never prosper."

"Them, either," he answered dully.

"Does your...does the Sno-Cat that came here have a heater in it?"

"Has a heater."

At the treeline, she began to get a stitch in her side. On the broad path of old glacier flow she stumbled and fell. He waited only long enough for her to get up before pressing on.

His pace would have been fine if she'd been on a jogging path. Slogging through snow to her knees over uneven, rocky ground was killing her. "Maybe we should just wait there for Jack to come."

"Jack to come." He shook his head violently. "No way, Jose. You have to go back. You have to go away. Jack has everything all mixed up."

"Gunnar, he doesn't really—"

"Doesn't matter. You have to go now."

More hopeless and exhausted than she had ever been in her life, she just wanted to lie down and die. Gunnar didn't want to know the truth about Mick. Watkins had befriended Gunnar, and that was all he knew or cared to know. Most of all, he didn't want to know, any more than anyone ever wanted to know, that he could have been so badly deceived.

The truth was, she couldn't blame Gunnar. With all their mental faculties to draw upon, most people didn't want to know or acknowledge the truth about themselves.

Not even Jack.

Not even her.

didn't want to know or acknowledge the truth about
themselves.
Not even Jack.
Not even her.

Chapter Nine

A bright lamp glowed inside the rectangular windows of an enormous, box-shaped Sno-Cat, creating an eerie oasis of light reflecting dimly off the vast expanse of frozen landscape. The logo on its door was that of the Silver Mountain Ski Association.

That the Sno-Cat had made it this far fed Jack's sense of disbelief. If he had thought it possible, he would have commandeered one of the all-terrain vehicles to complete the first leg of the rescue attempt, but no one in his right mind would have risked taking the Sno-Cat up an incline with a vertical drop half as severe as the other side of this mountain.

Gunnar Schmit was, however, clearly not in his right mind. He groomed ski trails by night for the ski area, and on his days off from the general store he took tourists on outings in Sno-Cats outfitted with seats. He had easy and unquestioned access to the powerful machines. Push come to shove, Gunnar was not only capable of operating the enormous tanklike vehicle, he was also uncomplicated enough in his thinking to believe he was entitled to its use.

And Jack had discounted the magnitude of Gunnar's loyalty to the friend he knew as Mick Hennessy. Believing Becky intended Mick harm, Gunnar must have hatched this plan to come after them and stop her.

When Gunnar Schmit took it into his head to do something, he didn't have the mental wherewithal to consider the range of consequences.

The muted rumble of the engine changed pitch, and the massive headlamps came on. Thrown into gear, the machine began to turn and crawl in the direction of Rampart. Jack took off skiing. He would have one chance to stop Gunnar, and only one—just before the Sno-Cat began its ascent of the mountainside.

In the open, he schussed down the snow-covered glacier flow. Following the aura of light glowing faintly through the relentlessly blowing snow, he had a downhill run all the way. Coming up behind the Sno-Cat in less than ten minutes, gauging Gunnar's course, Jack angled sharply to the left. When Gunnar began nosing up the mountain he had crossed to stop Becky, Jack would be standing directly in the path of the Sno-Cat, gambling with his life that Gunnar was not so far gone in his single-mindedness that he would run Jack down.

Poling powerfully, Telemarking his way up the first hundred feet of the slope, he climbed into the path of the Sno-Cat. Light beams more powerful than stage lights caught him full in the face.

He dropped his ski poles and backpack, rifle and all. The last thing he needed was to make Gunnar feel threatened in any way. He doffed his hat, peeled off his mask and stood in the path of the oncoming Sno-Cat, defenseless.

The huge machine ground to a halt, but neither the lights nor the engine went off. Squinting against the powerful lights, Jack could see nothing. A part of him had expected absolutely to be able to see Becky sitting in the Sno-Cat. He should have known Gunnar wasn't so simple as to give over his advantage and turn off the headlamps.

And in that instant, the fear invaded Jack that Gunnar was returning to Rampart alone. That to dismiss the threat Becky represented to his friend, Gunnar had left her unconscious to die of exposure along his route to the Sno-Cat.

He heard the pop of metal and knew Gunnar had opened his door. Knew he would kill Gunnar with his bare hands if he had left Becky for dead. If she was anywhere other than safe and warm in the cab of the Sno-Cat.

"You be gettin' out of the way, Jack Slade!" Gunnar called.

He held up a hand, blocking the worst of the glare. "Let her go, Gunnar." *Please, God, let him have her so he can let her go.*

"No dice, Jack! She ain't goin' nowhere but back to where she come from."

She was still alive, then. He unclenched his fists and closed his eyes. Relief swarmed through his body till he didn't know if he had it left in him to pull off dealing with Gunnar.

It was one thing to have recognized through all his jaded denials that she still meant something to him when nothing else did—and quite another to come this close to losing her. It was something else entirely to have his denials stripped clean.

Plumbing his last reserves, he girded his emotions to do what he had sworn he would never be called upon again to do.

To negotiate the release of a hostage.

To deliver a miracle when it had been made so desperately clear to him that Jack Slade was nothing if not fallible.

He strove for an unthreatening, dispassionate tone. "Come on, Gunnar. Don't be a jerk. Turn off that damned machine and we'll talk," he shouted over the engine noise.

"No talk, Jack," Gunnar shouted. "Ain't nothin' to talk about."

He shook his head, gambling that Gunnar would cave in to authority. "Turn it off, Gunnar."

"No way!"

"C'mon, man, you're blinding me! At least turn off the headlights." If he could only see her...

"You just better git outta the way, Jack," Gunnar

cried, frustrated, torn by old allegiances, wanting to please Jack, to be a friend in the midst of a conflict.

Jack shook his head. "It's not gonna happen, buddy. Not till you let her go."

"Not gonna happen. You got things all mixed up, Jack."

"Maybe I do, Gunnar, but we've been friends a long time, and I'm telling you we need to talk." A chill racked his body. "Maybe I have got things all mixed up," he went on. "Maybe you can straighten me out. But I'm only gonna say this one more time, buddy. Cut the lights. Do it now."

He had nothing with which to back his command, only whatever goodwill and respect he had built up with Gunnar over the years.

A long, tense moment went by. Rushing Gunnar would be a serious mistake, letting him think too much an even bigger mistake. Another thirty seconds passed before Gunnar complied and shut off the headlamps.

While his eyes adjusted, Jack let his head fall forward, let himself be grateful for small favors, for a chance, for a moment's respite in his fear of failing Becky.

When he could see again, when he saw Gunnar standing with one leg on the runner and Becky huddled in the cab, he shoved off on his skis, approaching the Sno-Cat, leaving his pack and rifle behind, even his ski poles.

Gunnar looked at him, his face a mask of ill-concealed hostility. "'m not listenin' to no b.s., Jack."

"I know that, Gunnar. I won't bullshit you. But I'm freezing my ass off out here."

"Freezin' my ass off," Gunnar repeated. He turned and yanked Becky through the space between the front seats into the jump seat behind him, then gave Jack a hand into the cab. He waited until Jack dropped into the seat still warm from Becky's body, then jerked a thumb toward the jump seat. "She's nothin' but bad news. Bad news."

"I can appreciate what you're saying, Gunnar, but she's a cop, and there'll be hell to pay if she winds up dead." He turned to look at her. What he saw made his heart twist. Her teeth chattered. Unable to stop shivering as her body warmed, she looked bruised, battered, utterly spent—and still utterly determined to prevail.

"Are you okay?"

"Yes." A deep, racking shudder passed through her. "I'll be fine now."

He nodded, reluctant to look away, wary of Gunnar sensing anything between them. He turned, forcing himself to ignore her, shaking his head for Gunnar's benefit, as if to agree that she was indeed nothing but a lot of bad news.

He had to appear to be wholly sympathetic with Gunnar's point of view to bring him around to his own. He thought Becky would understand that.

"I mean that, Gunnar." He peeled off his gloves

and tossed them on the floor, thrusting his hands toward the heater, making his body relax enough to absorb the warmth inside the cab. "If she hadn't come along when she did, just the wrong time, things probably wouldn't have gotten so screwed up."

"Damn straight," Gunnar intoned, wiping his nose on his sleeve. He had heard the words being bandied about in the bars.

"Damn straight," Jack echoed emphatically. "Trouble is, Gunnar, Mick is going to freeze to death out there if we don't get to him. Time is running out."

"Time is running out," he parroted. "It'll be her fault," Gunnar accused, jerking his thumb at Becky.

She started to interrupt. Jack shook his head to warn against it. "Think about this, Gunnar. It isn't going to matter whose fault it was. Mick will be just as dead. Is that what you want?"

"What you want? No," he snarled. "But you c'n go on. You don't need her. You make sure Mick don't die."

"Gunnar, I can't do it alone."

"You could if you wanted to, Jack Slade," Gunnar retorted sullenly. "You could."

"No, Gunnar. I couldn't. I need her, or I wouldn't have brought her along in the first place."

"Wait a minute!" He eyed Jack with sudden prurient suspicion. "I know what *you* want."

"Don't go there, Gunnar," Jack warned.

"Don't go there, Gunnar," he repeated nastily, his voice thickening as if he had been personally betrayed. "You don't care *nothin'* about Mick! You just want to boink her, Jack. You just want y'r fun, that's all. That's all."

Jack grimaced tightly. "If that's what I wanted, Gunnar, I sure as hell would not be here."

"Wouldn't be here, *bull*." Gunnar flushed angrily. "You sayin' you don't wanna boink her, Jack?"

He gave Gunnar a pissed, incredulous look. "Are you trying to pick a fight with me, Gunnar?"

"Hell, no." Gunnar backpedaled, confused and resentful.

"Well, you're about to get one." Jack pressed his advantage. "What's going on here? You think it's cool to be crude? When in the hell have you *ever* heard me spouting off about a woman like that?"

"Spouting off." Gunnar's jaw went up like a shot. "That time at the Ram you was cryin' in y'r beer. You was wishin' the hell you'd never been born." He jerked his head toward Becky. "She's the one, ain't she, Jack? She'd be the one you was cryin' about gettin' away? Ain't she, Jack?" Gunnar sneered. Two seconds before he'd been whining.

Heat flashed through him. Settled in his groin. He didn't remember the occasion, didn't want to think he'd ever gotten so stone-cold drunk as that, but Gunnar's uncharacteristic taunt had an overriding ring of truth about it.

Tempted to bullshit his way out of it with the dubious gift of his gilded tongue, he looked at Becky, started to shake his head, roll his eyes, act as if Gunnar had well and truly lost it.

He thought he could have pulled it off. If he hadn't been so goddamned tired, or if he could chuck whatever remained of his personal integrity, or if he had the balls to look her in the eye and lie like a son of a bitch. But even if he had the nerve, her eyes glittered with sudden tears, and she had her fisted fingers crammed tight against her trembling lips. He gave it up before he started down that slippery slope.

He looked at her another long moment. An awareness more acute than any memory of everything that had ever gone on between them surfaced. Lingered.

Her hand fell from her lips. Her face, so pale and drawn, flushed.

The heat flaring low in his body congealed.

He gritted his teeth and turned to Gunnar. "I won't lie to you, Gunnar. I never have, and I won't start now. So, yeah, she'd be the one."

"She'd be the one," Gunnar repeated. "You'd believe anything she says. You keep takin' her side."

"Whatever there was in the past between her and me doesn't change a thing, Gunnar. A man doesn't go spouting off about a woman like that. And I needed her help or I wouldn't have brought her with me. I still do."

He sat there unblinking, glaring at Jack.

"Gunnar, listen," Becky pleaded softly. "I know you don't trust me. I'm sorry that I lied to you. But you know you can trust Jack, don't you?"

"Trust Jack. Huh." His ruddy cheeks puffed resentfully.

"It might be better if you went with Jack," she continued reasonably. "You could be sure then that I couldn't harm Mick. But I can't manage to go back on my own, and someone's got to go for more help."

Jack sent her an appreciative glance. "That's right, Gunnar. Mick is going to have to be transported to Rampart."

"Maybe... Gunnar, do you think you could get this Sno-Cat thing close enough to bring Mick safely out? That way he won't have to wait for an evacuation team."

Gunnar cut her a long, mistrusting look.

"I swear to you, I won't hurt him."

"Swear to you," he echoed disdainfully. "Y'r word ain't worth squat. Y'r old man's a stinkin' drunk and y'r a bad news joke." He looked at Jack. "Gotta pay the piper. Pay the piper."

"Gunnar, that's enough," Jack snapped. "What the hell's gotten into you?"

"It's all right, Jack. It's true that I lied to Gunnar. And I...I told him about my dad. I—"

"Okay, look, Gunnar," Jack interrupted, his patience exhausted. "You can either go back and get

help or maneuver the Sno-Cat into a position to provide transport for the AirLife survivors to Rampart.
Which is it going to be?''

"You're not the boss of me, Jack.''

He shook his head slowly. "I'm just telling you,
Gunnar, that I'm taking Becky with me. You don't
have to like it. You don't have to show up. You
don't even have to go for help. Sooner or later, the
storm will break. But if there are survivors of that
crash, they're going to need water, at a bare minimum, or they will be dead. You choose.''

"You choose," Gunnar answered. He nodded.
"You say.''

"Fine. I'll go get my gear. You can take us to the
top of the glacier flow. We'll hike down to our
campsite. You make your way around the mountain
with the Sno-Cat until you find a way to the crash
site. Got it?''

Gunnar blinked. He turned his head oddly, like
an owl's, and stared at them each in turn. "Got it.''

"No more stunts, like snatching Becky, Gunnar,''
Jack warned.

"No more stunts, like snatching Becky," he repeated solemnly. "No more stunts like this.''

GUNNAR HAD GOTTEN them to within half a mile of
the ledge. Hiking the remaining distance to the snow
cave was an ordeal. Nightmarish, as if they had been
condemned to wander aimlessly through the heart of
a frozen no-man's-land in the dead of night.

But by eleven they were back to the ledge. The weight of new snow covered any trace of their work on the ledge—and of her struggle with Gunnar.

By the time Jack belayed her down the face of the cliff, she had long since passed the point of exhaustion, reaching a second wind, some unlikely place of strength or endurance within herself she had never experienced before or ever imagined.

They swept away the drift at the door to the snow cave. The wind howled fiercely, whipping up an even more dense cloud of snow than the blizzard itself produced.

Jack punched a vent hole through the ceiling with a ski pole. Becky took out a couple of candles, ordinary unscented wax in tins that could be closed. Moving silently, they fired up the miniature cookstove, then proceeded to consume pints of water and several packets of hearty rehydrated stew in the first hour.

The snow cave grew surprisingly warm. Stripped to her long underwear, Becky sat cross-legged on her sleeping bag, which was separated from the platform of snow by an insulating pad. Sipping from a mug of hot chocolate spiked with brandy, she asked, "Do you believe him, Jack?" When Jack didn't respond right away, she elaborated. "Gunnar, I mean. Do you believe he'll do as he promised?"

Propped against his pack on the cave floor, peeled to his long underwear, as well, Jack nodded. "I knew what you meant. What I don't know is whether I trust him or not. If anyone else said, 'No more stunts,' you could take it as agreement. Even a promise. But Gunnar repeats everything, so the only thing you know for sure is that he did hear you.'' Frowning, Jack twisted the cap off the fifth of brandy and took a long, warming pull. "I don't remember ever seeing Gunnar behave this way."

"Maybe it's me, Jack." She gave a small shrug. "I seem to push all his hot buttons."

"It's more than that, Becky."

He looked steadily at her. She found herself staring into the dregs of her hot chocolate. "More than what? Just me?"

"Or me."

She set aside her mug and forced herself to deal with the Pandora's box Gunnar had opened with his crude insinuations. The tension between her and Jack wouldn't go away because they ignored it. "Us, then?"

He gave a perfunctory nod, but there was nothing indifferent in the way he looked at her.

"I don't understand it."

Jack shook his head. The light of a candle glinted off the ruby stud in his ear, contrasting sharply with the masculine stubble of his unshaven jaw. The heat of danger and her deeply feminine vulnerability welled inside her.

"About the time you think you know Gunnar, something comes up and you find out how wrong you are. What blows me away is that at some level

Gunnar remembers everything he's ever heard. That he was able to draw the connection between you and—"

He broke off. His color deepened. His voice had dropped dangerously low, and she knew the keen sense of peril in going down this path had invaded him, as well.

He didn't finish. He didn't have to. She understood. He had once let his guard down under the influence of too many shots of a premium tequila and had let slip his regrets as to their breakup.

Worse still, he had let slip the extent of his pain, or unwittingly revealed himself to Gunnar, who couldn't process what anyone said until he repeated it for himself yet understood such things at a deeper level.

"I think it's even more than that, Jack. He reminded me of a Forrest Gump kind of personality from the very first."

Jack rolled his eyes.

"I know. Not a particularly tough call. But he does have the sort of animal instinct that hones right in on fear. I had hoped that Gunnar wouldn't understand that what I said I wanted with Mick, as opposed to what I really wanted, were two different things but he picked up on it. He may not be an intellectual giant, but he has this emotional radar that won't quit."

Jack sat there with his knees drawn up, his wrists

hanging off them, the flask of brandy dangling from his long fingers. "What are you getting at, Becky?"

"I'm not sure. If Watkins is on that downed AirLife chopper, he's in serious trouble. Even Gunnar should understand that if Watkins survived the crash uninjured, the cold could still kill him. The last thing we needed was to have to break away to deal with Gunnar's antics."

The urgency of their mission was never absent from her thoughts, or Jack's. The specter of crash victims surviving only to die of exposure made her skin crawl. "The longer it takes us to get to him—to any survivors—the worse their chances are. But…you know, I didn't get the feeling that Gunnar really gives a damn."

"Would you, if you were Gunnar?" He shook his head. "I don't think so. In his mind, you were clearly a bigger threat to Mick than freezing to death."

She shook her head. "I could buy that logic, Jack, if he hadn't decided to let me go. You heard him saying my word wasn't worth…what, squat? Why did he give up so easily?"

Jack raised his eyebrows. "I wouldn't have said he gave up easily."

"Okay," she conceded. "But what if we give Gunnar credit for realizing that I really am his enemy—or Mick's. And a worse one than time or the elements, because he understands at some uncanny level that in my heart, I would rather Michael Watkins—Mick—was not alive." She paused. Only the hiss of the gas in the cookstove disturbed the deep silence. "I'm so tired I can't see straight."

"I know. We both need some sleep."

"But I can't, Jack. There's something very wrong in all of this. I feel it. I think we ought to be asking ourselves *why* Gunnar would bother snatching me. Why waste time with either one of us? If he believed Mick was on that AirLife chopper, trapped and waiting for me to pick him off, then why didn't he try harder to beat us there and save his friend? And what was that crack about paying the piper?"

"I wondered about that myself. About all those things." Frowning thoughtfully, he tugged at his earlobe, fiddling with the half-carat ruby. He shrugged. "My best guess would be that he thought he was leveling the playing field by taking you out of the game. God only knows."

She gave a tired smile. "As if even God could know the mind of Gunnar Schmit."

"Exactly." His eyes, so dark in candlelight, fixed on hers.

She took a deep breath and sighed. "I don't know. It…he just seems to me to be really…*off*, you know? But I don't understand what makes Gunnar tick as well as you." She leaned down to spoon hot chocolate mix into her mug, then poured in hot water from the pot on the stove.

"Watkins obviously went to some lengths to endear himself to Gunnar," she went on, stirring her drink. "To have inspired that kind of allegiance. But Gunnar has the same kind of emotional attachment to you. I think he envies you."

The crease between Jack's brows deepened. "Envies what, exactly?"

"Come on, Jack." She straightened. Became suddenly, unaccountably...defensive. "You lead a devil-take-the-hindmost kind of life. You do what you want, when you want. You're not answerable to a woman...or a home and family. You don't even have to be accountable to yourself."

"Neither does he, Becky."

"But in a different way," she insisted. "You're everything he isn't, everything he can never be. A hotshot pilot, for example. The kind of man no woman willingly turns down." By the way he looked at her, then quickly looked away, by the angle of his jaw, the thudding of the pulse point in his neck, she knew he knew her deeper and more intimate meaning. That she, not any woman, would not have willingly turned away if he had shown himself to be the kind of man to hold himself accountable to himself and his woman.

His prolonged silence scared her. She chided herself. What could he say, after all? She cleared her throat and went on. "Gunnar admires you, Jack. He bragged to me that you used to be *the* hostage man for the FBI."

His expression a fierce, touching alloy of regret

and disbelief, Jack swore. "How would he know that?"

"I assumed you told him. He did admit you didn't want anyone else to know." She looked curiously at Jack. "Are you saying you don't remember telling him that?"

"I didn't," he replied stonily. "I wouldn't."

"Then why would he say that you had? How else would he know?"

"Beats the hell out of me." Small muscles thumped at his temple. "It's possible I may have spilled my guts about us. Even that I said your name. But not that. There was a time when I was proud of what I did, Becky. But after Highlands Creek—" He broke off and shook his head. "I didn't talk about it."

"Well. It doesn't really matter, does it?"

"I wish I believed that. With Gunnar, you're right. It probably doesn't matter. But I learned my lesson the hard way, that you can count on the one thing you ignored to come back and bite you in the butt."

"There is still the possibility I really am making mountains out of molehills."

Shaking his head, Jack frowned. "Let's think about this. If there's something off about Gunnar, it isn't that he realized Watkins would die of exposure but didn't give a damn. He cared about something enough to take that Sno-Cat over unrated terrain. And he might have seen you for the bigger threat to

Watkins's life when he started out, but something changed his mind, or—you're right—he wouldn't have let you go."

Becky agreed. "We have no clue, either, what he meant about paying the piper." She brainstormed a moment with variations. "Paying what? Paying up. Paying attention. Paying respects. Paying your dues. Payment on demand. Late payment. Paying...I don't know...paying the devil his due." A chill went through her with that one. "He'd just been saying my dad was a drunk and I was a joke." She swallowed. "In that context, it feels kind of personal."

"I'm sure it was meant to be, Becky, so far as Gunnar is capable of hidden agendas. You weren't going to go away, and from Gunnar's perspective, this rescue is about as phony as a two-dollar bill. In his eyes, you're a liar."

Her throat clutched. "Why does it matter to him? He knows you rescue people all the time. It's what you do. So when he thinks about this, why would he think the only reason you're out here is to have a quick and dirty bang with me somewhere in the wilderness?"

Jack's eyes darkened. He didn't like the sound of it coming from her mouth any more than he had liked it coming directly from Gunnar. He stared at his flask of brandy, brought it to his lips and took a long pull of the finely aged, premium liqueur. "Sounds crazy, doesn't it?"

"Jack, it *is* crazy. It doesn't make any sense.

What really changed after he realized I was the one you...you were talking about that night?''

Jack shook his head. He had a very bad feeling about what made sense to Gunnar Schmit. ''Maybe someday he'll tell us.''

Her voice was clotted with emotion. ''I can't believe he will be disloyal to you. He told me you know how to take care of things. That you always make the creeps who push him around back off and leave him alone.''

''Maybe.'' He took another swallow of brandy, a sort of cocky swig she didn't understand, looking at her over the bottle with that blue-flame intensity that made her mouth go dry, made her breasts tighten and feel heavy. ''But, as usual, you confuse the truth with the facts. Standing up for a half-wit doesn't make a hero, Becky.''

Chapter Ten

"Don't even dare to try suggesting to me what makes a hero, Jack. I'm so...I mean..." Her hand fluttered wearily over her eyes. "I'm so tired of all your hypocritical quibbling. I won't fight with you."

"Good idea." He sat for long seconds looking at her. "I wish things had gone differently between us, Becky."

"I wished so, too."

"I knew that."

"Did you have to act like you couldn't really have cared less?"

"At the time?" He swallowed. "Yeah. I did. I didn't know how else to get through your breaking it off between us."

"I loved you, Slade." Her throat tightened. "I told myself I didn't. Not...not really. I told myself that you would move on as constantly advertised." She hesitated, stared into her mug, then met his gaze again. "But I did. I loved even the way you looked at me. Like—" She broke off.

It was true she was too tired to be thinking straight, too bruised and battered and worn to be having this conversation. But she had withheld the truth of her feelings for him four years ago, and whether it was the right thing to do or not, keeping her feelings to herself had cost her dearly. "Like you're looking at me right now."

He sat no more than a couple of feet from her. The scent of hot wax and chocolate, of brandy and their heated bodies filled the pocket of air they breathed. The candles burned without so much as a flicker, reflecting off the pure white snow.

By contrast, Jack loomed larger, seemed darker, harder, more male, more a threat to her heart and restraint and equilibrium than she could possibly counter.

"How am I looking at you, Becky?" A heartbeat marked her silence, then another. "Tell me. Say it," he demanded.

"As if—" No one in her life had ever looked at Becky with the kind of abiding respect for her she found in Jack's eyes. The kind of respect that acknowledged his deep flaws and that said he knew all about her flaws, as well, and cared deeply for her anyway.

She had no nerve left to pluck up, no more emotional endurance. Simply, artlessly, she acquiesced. "As if you know a part of you touches a part of me where no one has ever thought to reach for before."

She had never opened herself so far or been so scared. "Like shadows touching hands."

"'Bleeker Street.'"

She nodded. She still had his Simon and Garfunkel CDs. A tension hung in the air, tinged with the scent and feel of a world contained in a snow cave they had built together where old feelings provoked a still deeper intimacy.

I saw a shadow touch a shadow's hand. He lost his nerve. Broke off their eye contact.

"Jack, you risked your life out there tonight for me. What does that say to you?"

He shook his head, and adopted her self-defensive tactic of making a joke of it. "Not to put too fine a point on it, Becky, but there was no way Gunnar was going to run me down."

"You know what I mean." She lowered her voice. "You did what you had to do to stop Gunnar. And then you got him to think again about what he was doing. No matter how he feels about me, he respects you too much to keep making this whole thing a contest of wills or loyalties. You treat him with respect. You deal with him as a fellow human being."

"None of that matters in the end, Beck. People will do what they want to do. Gunnar stopped because, at some level, he already knew what he was doing was wrong."

"Say it doesn't matter all the way to kingdom come if you want. I don't believe you. People do act according to their own agendas, yes. We all want what we want, but so what? What you do, what anyone does, speaks a lot louder than what you say.''

They had never talked about what had happened to her as a little girl, never talked about her father. She knew only that his dad was a preacher, and that he'd rejected the preacher's son, bad-boy pigeonhole as much as its goody-two-shoes opposite.

She hadn't bared her soul. He hadn't bared his. They were both too private. Spending hours on end together, they had made love in many ways save the act itself. She was only beginning to understand, all these years later, what a tribute to their relationship abstaining had been, what it meant now.

There were serious gaps in what they knew about each other's lives—which was probably what had made it all so seemingly effortless to move on, behaving as if all they'd ever meant to each other could be summed up as a casual flirtation.

It wasn't.

''Do you want to know when it was that I really fell in love with you?''

''No.''

''Jack.''

''What would be the point, Becky?''

She ignored his implicit warning against straying into such territory. ''It was the day I figured out why you're so brilliant at hostage negotiations.''

His jaw tightened. In the scant candlelight, his

face was mottled with a dangerous emotion, another powerful admonition.

She refused to let it go. "It's because, just like with Gunnar, no matter how desperate the situation, you never lost sight of the fact that you were dealing with another human being. Someone who wasn't born into the world spoiling to take anyone else out of it."

"Yeah. Hey, we're all God's children, doin' the best we can."

"Why do you make fun of it?" she cried. His jaded expression drew her anger like talons draw blood. "People have been killing each other off for a very long time, Jack. You're not personally responsible."

He tightened his jaw and bent his head. When he looked up at her, his eyes were dulled. "So are you're saying now that God *didn't* just invent the hostage genre for me to show off?"

The biting sarcasm, aimed at himself, stole her breath away. The grief weighing on his soul hadn't abated in four long years. Her throat convulsed. "Jack."

"Becky." He looked at the pristine white ceiling of the snow cave and sighed deeply. "Why don't you just ask it?"

"Ask what?"

"If Gunnar is right. Whether it's true that all I really want with you is a good f—"

"Stop it, Jack!" she cried, clapping her hands over her ears.

It wasn't that she didn't know, hadn't herself heard or even used the word he intended in times of deep upset. But even Gunnar hadn't dared used the word. Jack not only dared, but the devastating speed, the changing of the subject, the moving in for the kill to avoid his overwhelming emotions, shoved her up against a wall.

Staring into his flinty eyes, dismayed and disoriented, she knew that was exactly what he had intended, what he meant her to feel.

He couldn't make her accept the truth of the gospel according to Jack. He couldn't bully her into seeing him in the same disregard as he saw himself. But he had found a way to disabuse her of her illusions once and for all.

He must believe she would finally see the light of day and bolt if only he could manage to humiliate her or sufficiently demean what was between them.

He was wrong.

Her instinct for self-preservation demanded she keep her mouth shut and turn away from him. To forget or reject or deny altogether that she loved him or that she could ever have loved Jack Slade.

He would as soon see her chew off a limb like a wild she-wolf caught in the fierce steel jaws of a trap as remain caught herself in the trap of loving him.

But she would rather die than maim herself in

that way only to suit his jaundiced opinion. She pulled her legs close to her body and rested her chin on her silk-clad knees.

"What is it, Jack?" she asked softly. "Do I strike you as a fair-weather friend? Do I seem to you to be the kind of woman to turn tail and run like a rabbit because you snarl at me?"

GORDY KUBIAK tried the residence of Louis Difalco from the courtesy phones in the patients' family waiting room of the intensive care unit. The phone rang at least twenty, probably thirty times before Gordy gave up, broke off, dialed the number again to make sure he hadn't misdialed, and got the same response.

He recalled the address from having looked up the telephone number. The house number on South Pearl Street told him Becky's dad lived in an apartment house in the thick of a neighborhood infamous for trouble.

The foot traffic coming out of the Mexican restaurant and cantina across the street guaranteed sleepless nights. Sirens screamed by a couple of times per night.

Not a neighborhood, Gordy reflected, that he would choose to frequent given most any alternative. The locals had a nose for cops of any stripe and no particular fondness for them, either. But it came down to picking his way there through streets piled four feet high with snow and broken branches, littered with stranded vehicles, or failing to bring Difalco in per Aguilar's instructions.

He arrived at the Difalco address four hours and some odd minutes after he began trying to reach Becky's old man by phone.

The building was shaped like a sawed-off box of saltines. Once upon a time it had sported the latest in security measures, but that time was probably forty years ago, long since gone. Gordy got past the security doors as if one were supposed to walk on in and walked up the three stories in a dark and dingy stairwell surprisingly free of graffiti.

He pounded on the door. "Mr. Difalco? Sir? You in there?"

He got no answer. He pounded on the door for five, maybe seven minutes, then decided to check out the cantina across the street on the chance he'd find Difalco hunched over a drink at the bar.

Difalco wasn't there. What Gordy got was a lot of lip and a ration of attitude of the who's-asking variety from the patrons. They'd pinned him for a cop, and they gave up nothing but contradictory stories.

Difalco being ex-FBI, the closed-mouth loyalty he commanded in the cantina surprised Gordy. Maybe he shouldn't be surprised, though. Maybe a washed-up, has-been cop fitted in with these lowlifes just fine.

In any case, no one had seen him in three, maybe four days.

Come to think of it, that was an unusually long time not to see Louie hangin' around.

Gordy trudged across the street feeling uneasy. It was impossible to tell whether the sentiment was genuine concern or a gibe of which Gordy was the butt.

Again at Difalco's door, he made a commotion loud enough to raise the dead. The fleeting thought came and went that Difalco might just be dead. Gordy gave one sharp shove with his shoulder and the lock gave. The doorjamb splintered.

Louis Difalco sat passed out cold in an alcoholic stupor. Gordy's stomach turned. He wanted to hold his nose. The stench of Scotch hung on every surface and molecule of oxygen in the air.

It took an hour to rouse the man, throw him in the shower and get enough instant coffee down his gullet to render him halfway coherent.

Louis Difalco didn't even ask where he was being taken till they hit the street. "Is this about the train derailment?" he asked.

Gordy nodded grimly. "That's the least of it, sir." It was, Gordy knew, a damn good reason for Difalco to have gotten drunk off his butt if he had registered the signature of Michael Watkins all over the disastrous derailment. Louis Difalco wore his failure, his guilt, like a second skin.

Joe Aguilar's question to Difalco would be one more truly nasty shock.

THE SILENCE inside the cave of snow was so complete, so uneasily natural, that he imagined he could hear her nervous swallow, hear her pulse thudding, hear his heart knocking senselessly about.

A stillness took hold of Jack, the frozen instant in time just before the battle was to be engaged when one must win and the other lose.

After he answered, nothing would ever be the same between them again, for good or ill. Here was his chance. This was the moment. He had it within his control to make her turn tail in spite of herself and take all her high-flown expectations with her.

"Jack?"

His brow creased. He shook his head. Saliva pooled in his mouth. He felt as utterly incapable of driving her away as he was unfit to encourage her in any way. After the devastation at the Highlands Creek Middle School, he had learned and applied, quite ruthlessly ever after, the skill of cauterizing emotion from his soul as efficiently as if it were gangrene taking a limb.

Any emotion. Grief, self-loathing, self-respect, love. *Stoke up the fire, Slade. Heat the iron to white-hot. Cauterize. Better charred than cheered, better scarred than scared shitless.*

Becky both cheered and scared him shitless with her bedrock faith in his character, and God help him, he couldn't remember how to pull the iron from the fire, much less apply it to the emotion she drew from him.

He met her dark eyes. "I don't know what you want from me, Becky."

"An answer. The truth." She forced herself to keep eye contact. "Whether or not all you want from me is as Gunnar said it was. I am not a fair-weather friend, Jack, but I'm not a martyr, either."

He gave a shaky sigh. His voice was reduced to a harsh whisper. "If sex was all I wanted from you, I would have had it a long time ago."

Her breath locked in her throat. Her gaze darted away. It was just the sort of swaggering, macho, asshole assumption that he would have had it if he'd wanted it that would finally have made his case, that would have finally labeled him an irredeemable bastard.

He couldn't do it, couldn't leave it alone, couldn't stand for her to cave in and accept the version of Jack Slade that faithfully fulfilled every one of his father's harsh pronouncements.

"It would have been fine while it lasted, but it would have been long since over between us."

Tears sprang to her eyes. She pressed her lips tight to stop the trembling. "I have to know what you mean, Jack. You have to be clear with me. Are you saying it isn't over for you...between us?"

His gaze left her, settled low, came back. "If you're asking me is it sex I want, the answer is...obvious. But if you're asking me—" his already gravelly voice dropped an octave "—if sex is all that I want from you?'' Slowly, he shook his head. ''The answer is no. It isn't over.''

Relief swarmed over him. His father, the Reverend Slade, liar that *he* was, had knocked Jack around for fifteen years to make this very point. That to tell the truth, all of it, made the years of necessary lies quite unnecessary, after all.

''It's funny,'' he said, staring at his hands, hating them, realizing how much they reminded him of his father's hands. ''With my old man, telling the truth was only an invitation to more grief.'' Which, he thought, had the nasty effect of molding him into a terribly efficient liar where his feelings were concerned. So clever that until thirty seconds ago, he hadn't quite managed even to tell himself the truth.

He looked up from his hands. ''I can't make promises, Becky. It would be a serious mistake to confuse the truth for the facts again.''

She straightened, giving her head a shake, refusing, he thought, to listen to his litany of warnings.

She lowered her legs, rose from the pallet of snow, then knelt on her coat before the cookstove. ''When I was a little girl, I thought everybody told the truth but me.''

She dipped a washcloth into the pot of hot water. She squeezed out the excess water with both hands, then brought the warm, wet cloth to her face. ''Fibs, really, if you take into account the severity. I once hid a stuffed turtle that belonged to my cousin under my bed so she would forget to take it home. She didn't forget, though. My mom asked me if I knew where George was, and I stood there and lied right through my baby teeth.''

Sitting sideways in front of him, she seemed focused on the memory. She gave a distant smile tinged by regret. But she drew the warm, wet cloth slowly, languidly over her cheek, down her neck, pausing over her collarbone, coming to rest at the top of her breast.

His blood began to grow thick, to pool.

She looked at him. "That's the first time I remember knowing that I was lying. I thought—'' she broke off, shaking her head, smiling at herself ''—I thought I had invented the very act of lying.'' She drew the cloth across the tops of her breasts. "And that I must be a very...naughty little girl.''

He swallowed spit to assure himself he would not swallow his own tongue. "What happened?''

"All hell broke loose.'' She soaked the washcloth again, went through the same languorous motions on the other side. "My mother went straight to my bed and pulled George out from underneath.''

He shook his head. He watched her fingers dip into the sides of the neckline of her silk top. Felt his sex thickening. Was it possible she didn't know her effect on him? "How did she know?''

"My mother had eyes in the back of her head. By the time she was done scolding, I just wanted to slip through the cracks in the floor and disappear.''

He knew the feeling. Remembered all the ways

the Reverend had in his repertory of taking a kid apart for being a kid. "She couldn't have had much on my father."

She gave a bittersweet half smile. "No. I don't suppose she had. But the point is that I hated her for that, Jack, and I wished, cross my heart and hope to die, with all my heart, *fiercely,* that she was dead. And guess what?"

He could hear it coming.

Her hand stilled over her breast. She gave a small, desperate nod. She shook off the memory and breathed deeply. She rinsed the cloth again, wrung it out. "Before the sun went down that day, my mother *was* dead."

There wasn't a kid who ever lived and breathed who hadn't wished the same thing. He knew she knew it, and so he said nothing.

She swallowed hard. "I was only five, Jack, and I believed I *was* the only child alive to ever have lied, the only one who ever wished one of her parents was dead, and then to get my careless wish..." She met his eyes. "You have to admit, not many five-year-olds get that wish. So it was only natural to believe it was all my fault that she died."

"Didn't your father—"

"No," she interrupted fiercely. Louis Difalco had wallowed too deep in pain and liquor to help her see it wasn't her fault. It was his friends' wives who had taken her to the procession of doctors, the ones who concluded she would never again believe in a benevolent world. "He didn't. But I don't want to talk about my father."

Alarms went off in Jack's head, warnings of something desperately wrong. "Maybe you should, Becky."

"Maybe." Still, by her expression he could tell she'd dismissed the subject of her father. "But I only brought it all up because it's the same magical thinking as wishing the cornice of snow will fall and bury Michael Watkins alive. That if I wish it hard enough, it will happen." Her hand slipped beneath the hem of her silk top and climbed slowly upward.

His breath caught. His throat locked. He watched her bathing her breasts, her gaze falling to his thickened sex so obvious beneath the soft cotton long johns he wore.

Her eyes flared. She blinked once, and again, and he knew then that she had intended from the first to have the effect she was having on him.

He shut his eyes and leaned his head against the wall of snow. She'd had a rotten childhood.

So had he.

So had a lot of others. But he didn't think, sitting so near to him and bathing herself in the soft glow of candlelight in a snow cave in a Colorado blizzard, intending, he believed, to arouse him, that a child's magical thinking or a rotten childhood was her point.

His body thrummed. So heated and full, swollen tight with the want of her beneath the worn soft cotton cloth of his long johns, he drew a shaky breath and waited for her, watching her.

She finished bathing her body. He knew from the mottled shadows on the snow cave wall exactly when she stripped off her top and bottoms, when she replaced her top with one that brushed her thighs, when she emptied the water and filled the pan with bricks of snow, prattling on…and how she failed to draw on another pair of silken long johns.

She soaked a fresh cloth, stepped with one foot over his legs and sat straddling his thighs.

Desire tore through him like a flash flood in a desert canyon a thousand feet deep and two feet wide. He thought to warn her.

He thought again.

HIS HANDS were splayed on her hips, and he brought his powerful thighs upward till she slipped naked to the juncture of his legs, till she slid still more intimately astride him. Her sweet cry of surprise, of startling pleasure, rippled through his body.

If he had a coherent word to say, it would not be a warning. What would be the use, when his sex bulged thick and hard and hot between her parted legs?

She began to wash his face, holding his hair against his scalp. It was all he could do and more—with the cold flesh of her bottom beneath his hands and the damp, warm, feminine core of her already parted over him—to bear her gentle, almost maternal ministrations.

"I believed, Jack."

"In what?" He had lost track.

"I believed in my power to wish a thing and have it come true." She put down the warm cloth and stripped off his long underwear shirt as if he were a small boy.

Her reserve slipped then.

Slipped badly.

Slipped, finally, altogether.

Her beautiful dark eyes flared, and she forgot to pick up her cloth before she touched him. The fingers of both hands stroked his silky dark hair and shaped themselves to his pecs.

Her low, throaty moan strummed his sex like the shaft of an arrow pulled powerfully back along the strings of a bow drawn taut, and though she shuddered and cried out as a hot tide poured out of her, bathing his throbbing sex, she distracted herself, picking up the cloth and dipping into the hot water again, wringing out the cloth, placing it flat on his chest.

She swallowed and looked at his face. "It took a long time for me to figure out that I wasn't the only one. That people don't always tell the truth. People *show* you the truth by what they do. And what they show you is what you can believe."

He thought—as far as he could think in the state he was in—that he finally understood her, finally got what her small tale of childish behavior had been about.

What she said confirmed what he knew. "I don't want your promises, Jack. I want you to show me who you are. Who we are together."

Her husky plea touched off a burst of hot desire, a thrusting of his sex beneath her, an arousal gone beyond turning back.

Cradling her hips in his hands, caressing the hollows beneath the crests of her pelvis, he brought his lips to the curve of her jaw and the smooth, delicate flesh below. The tip of his tongue stroked her skin, probing at the pulse point in her neck till the thudding of her heartbeat matched the pulsing in his groin.

A longing unfurled low in her body, and she strained toward him, exposing still more of her neck to his lips, more of her being to his taking, but he groaned and withdrew and touched his tongue for a devastating instant to her breast instead.

The damp imprint left by his marauding tongue cooled. Her nipples drew taut. Unbearable pleasure, bestowed and then stolen away, ricocheted through all her senses. He smelled of soap and brandy. She could so nearly feel the heat of the powerful elixir on her breast. Fixed on the shapes of her breasts, on the tautness, his eyes dilated, flared, shuttered. He closed them with a groan that reverberated in her soul.

His hands stroked her torso, ending just below the

fullness of the sides of her breasts, ending far short, deliberately, maddeningly shy of possession or even a caress. Her exquisite frustration came out in a broken cry and shook him to the core.

"Becky." He raised his mouth to hers. She raised her arms to expose herself to his hands and cradle his face in hers. She wanted his kiss quite desperately, the taste of his hot breath, the tang, the wet, but most of all, the reassurance of him.

She could bear the fullness and aching of her breasts for his touch if only she could have the reassurance of his kiss to let her know the man she loved still resided in the body and soul of Jack Slade.

He groaned deeply and opened his mouth to her, and sensation after sensation of heat and home, of sweetness and bitter years of absence, of abstinence, rolled through her body, a passion all but forgotten roused in her in its wake, flushing her skin, swelling her lips, banishing the loneliness she only distantly recognized she had suffered so dearly.

Jack sensed the yielding of all constraint in her, sensed her emptiness and hunger. Somewhere deep in his soul he understood that only he could ever fill those hidden ravines. The sense of her acquiescing and demanding he meet her there in those deep, secret spaces went through his body in wild ripples of pleasure.

He filled his hands with her breasts, stroked the

taut buds of her nipples, suckled at her tongue and her lips, swallowed her muted cries.

She sank lower, harder against his swollen sex, and the moisture that flowed out of her, over him, eroded for all time his resistance.

He shifted beneath her. It might have been so simple, the shifting of his weight, but it wasn't—and she knew it—and a wild, deeply feminine joy over her power to dispel his control rose like a phoenix from the stone-cold ashes inside her.

And when he freed himself and she took him inside her, she looked into his eyes. "I gave up wishing for anything for a long time. This is the only thing, Jack," she whispered, looking deeper into his eyes, "that I ever dared wish for so hard I imagined it must come true."

Like the impenetrable walls of Jericho his father had invoked in his sermons a thousand times or more, against the onslaught of Becky's love, Jack's almighty defenses crumbled.

Chapter Eleven

In the intensive care unit, where his daughter's superior in the Colorado Bureau of Investigation lay fighting a massive coronary, Louis Difalco entered fighting his own battle.

It wasn't a new one, only a new twist of the knife in his gut. In twenty-five years, he had refused to let down his guard. He had always known the world would hear from Michael Watkins again, and now it had.

He took a moment before stepping inside Aguilar's unit to screw up his courage, but Kubiak was breathing down his neck. Squaring his shoulders, he took the few short steps to Aguilar's bedside.

"Joe."

Aguilar opened his eyes, blinked tiredly, breathed deeply. "Louie."

"How're you doing?"

Aguilar's eyes flicked away, not soon enough to conceal rank disdain. "I'll be fine."

Louis wondered how, after all these years of enduring the morass of his own self-contempt, Aguilar's scorn still had the power to make his gut burn. "You have something to say to me, Aguilar, spit it out."

Aguilar briefly closed his eyes, then signaled Kubiak to elevate the head of his bed. "Does he know?"

Kubiak operated the electric controls and shook his head. Aguilar nodded and turned to Louis.

Annoyed, Louis demanded, "Know what?"

Kubiak piped up. "During the early morning hours, shortly before the train derailed, all the computers in the CBI network froze on the image of a gravestone."

"Not just any gravestone, Louie," Aguilar added, his eyes half-closed. "This was Maeve's gravestone."

"Maeve." A frisson of foreboding climbed Louis's backbone. "It was Watkins, then."

"I'd say that's a safe bet." Aguilar looked away again. Was it anger more than contempt? "Why do you think Watkins would use an image of Maeve's gravestone?"

Louis found that he didn't want to think why. "What the hell difference does it make? He needed some way to lead you by the nose and let you know he was responsible. He accomplished that. You now know he did it. He blew up the goddamn train, and that's probably not all he has in mind."

Aguilar ripped the oxygen mask off his head. His

hair stood up at ridiculous angles, both arms were stuck with IVs, his pallor was deadly. But despite all those signs of weakness, apparent or real, Louis found himself feeling threatened, stepping back.

"Yeah, he blew up the goddamn train," Aguilar snapped, "and yeah, I can freaking guarantee you that's not all. But I'm the only one who knew who the hell Maeve Hennessy was, and so I am also telling you this. By using her gravestone for a signature, he ran the unnecessary risk of his train wreck going unaccounted for."

"That's ridiculous," Louis protested. "He's playing meaningless games with you. Sooner or later someone—"

"Watkins would not take such an unnecessary risk unless he meant more than to claim the derailment," Aguilar interrupted, brushing aside Louis's protest as he would the annoying buzz of a mosquito. "Nor were his games ever *meaningless*." He swore in his native Spanish. "My patience is running thin. I'm asking you, *Louis*," his emphasis conveying thick disdain "—why he used Maeve's gravestone."

"I'm telling you, *I don't know*."

"Could it be that this is the anniversary of Maeve's death?"

Louis knew the urge to throw up like he knew the urge to take a piss. In the last half of his misbegotten, drunken life, vomiting was that routine. He felt the urge now, even if he didn't understand, stone-cold sober, where it might be coming from. "I suppose it could."

Aguilar took a hit of oxygen from the green-hued plastic mask in his hand, then went relentlessly on. "Could it be, Louis, that Michael Watkins is not done avenging the murder of his beloved Maeve?"

Louis grimaced. "Maeve Hennessy wasn't murdered. She was hit by a stray bullet or a ricochet, and the reason she died at all was—"

"Could it be," Aguilar interrupted, ignoring the correction of fact, "that Watkins did not consider the score with you settled by the crude and untimely manner of your wife's death?"

Louis swore. "What the hell are you getting at, Aguilar? You want to blame me for this, go right ahead. I let him get away, and twenty-five years later you still want to make me the scapegoat, fine. But—"

"Could it be, Louis," Aguilar interrupted one last time, "that Michael Watkins will settle for nothing less than the life of your daughter?"

"Becky?" Louis felt the tide of the blood in his head and face running opposite the surge of bile scalding his throat. "What does she have to do with this? What the hell have you done? Did you...is she—" He could barely squeeze the heinous thought into words, let alone get the words past his throat. "Has he got her?"

Aguilar's contempt multiplied and shone in his eyes. "She's gone after him."

"Why? For God's sake, why?" Louis demanded harshly.

"Why Becky, you mean?" Aguilar asked. "You tell me. Go ahead, Louis. Make your case one more time. Tell me again how Maeve died. Maybe this time it will make sense of why Watkins took his revenge on your family—"

"One thing has nothing to do with another—"

"—and why," Aguilar continued, gasping for breath, refusing to ease his tormented heart and lungs before making his point, "*why* Michael Watkins went to such lengths to involve your daughter and make sure all responsibility for stopping him this time stopped with her."

Louis felt himself coming apart at his tenuous seams, felt himself retching, dry-heaving inside. No autopsy was ever performed, no bullet ever extracted from the brain of Maeve Hennessy.

No one would ever know.

No forensic comparison of bullet to gun barrel would ever expose her deliberate murder, yet Louis felt his brilliantly crafted, carefully constructed, meticulously maintained justification…unraveling.

Someone needed to pay. Too many lives had been lost.

Visions flitted through his head like an old-fashioned spool of film gone berserk and replaying for his mind's eye what he had refused to see outside his nightmares in all the years since.

He saw Michael Watkins in the frenzied final seconds before he disappeared, saw him laughing, saw him blowing a kiss to the beautiful flame-haired daughter of a federal district court judge....

Maeve Hennessy, paying her father back for God only knew what perceived humiliations, too young to know better, had played decoy quite brilliantly, enabling Watkins's escape.

Louis saw himself on the film in his mind's eye, a man of fundamental, unquestioned, hard-ass, bedrock values. A man who would no more take the law into his own hands than he would fire on an innocent bystander.

He saw his younger self corrupted in an instant, in the split second of rage when he knew Watkins would make another clean getaway. And he watched himself turning, pulling his firearm and drawing a bead on the flame-haired head of the judge's beautiful daughter.

And then, quite apart from the imagined spool of silent film, he heard himself warning Watkins.

Someone's got to pay the piper, Mick....

Louis fell to his knees, but if he meant to pray for mercy or for a heart attack like Aguilar's to put him out of his misery, he gave it up for a lost cause. To hear Aguilar's condemnation was to hear out loud what Louis had always known, what had turned him more certainly to drink than his own wife's death.

It would never be proven, inside or outside a court of law, but there wasn't one of Louis Difalco's peers who believed the bullet that killed Maeve Hennessy hadn't come straight and true from his sidearm.

Someone's got to pay.

IN THE OFFICES of the Colorado Bureau of Investigation, the computers flickered briefly, went dark, then came slowly to light. This time the image was of a plant of some sort or other. It was the switchboard operator Joe Aguilar considered to be incompetent who, having been raised in the South, recognized the mint leaves, and Sorenson, the much-beleaguered shift supervisor, who first suggested that the United States Mint in Denver be evacuated and a bomb squad brought in.

At the corner of the image, a clock ticked down the passing seconds. The time remaining stood at T minus nine hours twenty-five minutes and thirty-six seconds.

Plenty of time to find and destroy a bomb.

But everyone involved understood this was almost certainly no ordinary explosive for which the bomb-squad dogs or their trainers were adequately prepared.

Michael Watkins was not known to give notice, and the fact that he had—and set the clock so precisely—only meant he had every reason to expect a warning would serve no purpose but to rattle their cages moment by moment.

THEY SLEPT for no more than three, maybe three and a half hours. Becky dressed and cooked rehydrated eggs, hash brown potatoes and canned bacon, while Jack made a quick visual search in a hundred-and-twenty-degree arc for any evidence off the downed medevac chopper.

When he crawled into the cave covered with snow, she turned off the gas burners and began serving the food.

"Smells good. I could eat a bear."

"Sorry, no bears." She waited until he had stripped off his coat, then handed him a tin plate and fork. "Just eggs and bacon and potatoes. Any sign of the crash?"

He nodded grimly, stuffing his mouth. He chewed and swallowed in short order. "The snow drifting like it is distorts the shape of everything, but I did spot what appears to be the tail rotor sticking out of the ravine."

"We're that close, then?"

Polishing off another mouthful, he nodded. "Close enough to see, yeah."

"What about the cornice?"

"Can't see it, but that's—"

"To be expected," she said. "We won't see it from below either, will we?"

"No." He smirked. "Not unless it gives way."

"Oh, that's very funny, Jack."

"Becky." He stopped wolfing his food long enough to put down his fork, reach out and cup her cheek. "Just a little gallows humor. I don't know what it's going to take to get to the chopper, but we have to hurry.''

Before the cornice did give way, she thought. She nodded, scooping eggs onto her fork. The tension between them sprang not from careless fanciful promises in the face of a situation in which it was possible neither one of them would survive, but from a sense of possibilities that had not existed before between them.

The uncertainty of any future sharpened their senses, put all their possibilities into an equally uncertain context. The only rational course was to set aside everything but dealing with whatever they would find at the crash site.

She forced down her plateful and served the last of the eggs and bacon to Jack, then took a couple of minutes to wash the dishes in the pot of hot water and to get herself mentally prepared.

She dressed quickly again in layers, drew on her boots and coat and scooted on her bottom down through the narrow opening of the cave. The wind blew as fiercely as it had for the past two days, whipping snow furiously about. Jack had placed her cross-country skis just a few steps away, and while he harnessed himself to the sled, she lashed on her skis.

They covered the distance to the shallow ravine in half an hour, but what had appeared to Jack from a distance to be the tail rotor sticking up from the ravine was actually the tail rotor broken off and wedged where it had fallen. Below, in the ravine where they had expected to find the downed helicopter, there was nothing.

Jack dropped to his haunches to shove the sled harness over his head. He remained hunkered, trying to figure out where the body of the chopper had gone down.

Becky made her way to his side. "How is this possible? Where can it be?"

Jack shook his head and rose. "Not very far." He scanned what could be seen of the horizon in small, intense segments. "Are you all right with separating?"

"On a search pattern?" She nodded.

"The fuselage can't be far, Becky, but visibility being what it is, we'll need to be almost on top of it before we see it."

"Jack, I'm okay with separate searches."

"Okay. Well..." He grimaced. "I'm not okay with it."

She looked at him. A part of her knew there was no way he could treat her like an ordinary rescue personnel taking equal risks as if nothing had happened between them. "Tell me you aren't going to start second-guessing me now."

He swore under his breath. "Becky, this is not just any rescue, and you know it. Not with Michael Watkins at the end of it."

"This is just like any other rescue, Jack, right up until it's not. We do what we have to do, we do it safely, we bring the survivors home, and we don't take stupid risks. I won't be stupid."

"If you find the fuselage, you don't go near it. Not until you're with me," he ordered. "You don't call out, you don't make yourself known, you don't yell for me, you don't sneeze. You turn around and you come back. Clear?"

"Clear." She knew exactly what he meant and why he thought it necessary to drill it into her head. There was still the inconceivable chance that Watkins had not only survived, but lay poised in wait for her. "Can I have the compass now?"

"No." He wanted to plant her here, keep her safe, keep her from danger, keep her for himself. If anything happened to her, he would tear up the earth. If he had ever had to do anything harder than letting her go off on her own right now, he didn't know what it was or when. He swallowed hard. "You're taking the GPS."

"Okay. Can I have the GPS now?"

He handed her the small unit. "Keep to the thirty-degree vector. I'll take due north. Watch the time. We'll meet back here in one hour, so don't go more than twenty or twenty-five minutes before turning around."

She nodded. "I'll be here, Jack. Right here." She turned away, more fearful of the portent of a hug than of confronting Watkins, and began skiing on her search vector. Pausing every few minutes, she scanned the surrounding landscape. Ten minutes into her allotted search time, skiing along on an ever-narrowing ledge, she spotted the twisted wreckage covered with a foot-thick layer of snow.

Already stopped, she went so still as not to breathe. The main rotor was bent wildly askew, and the body of the helicopter had suffered accordionlike folds. The top, at her eye level, seemed sheered off or compacted, but with the drifting, it was impossible to tell which.

Becky shuddered. It would be a miracle if anyone had survived. Even Watkins, she thought. Surely even he could not have survived.

The wreckage lay about fifteen degrees off her course to the north. She supposed it was possible Jack could have spotted the body of the crashed helicopter from his vantage point, but if he had been able to keep strictly to a due north course, he would come out high above the site and almost certainly directly below the cornice. The side of the mountain rose to her right at an impossibly steep pitch.

She checked her watch. Taking the last few remaining minutes before she must turn back, she looked for any signs of life. A depression, perhaps, in the snow atop the crash that would indicate melting due to warm air rising from inside.

She saw nothing. Heard nothing. Turning back, she saw the dark shape of a man coming toward her. Jack.

Yes. It was Jack.

He approached her silently. She held up her thumb, pointing backward. He nodded.

He drew up close beside her, ducked out of the harness and spoke softly. "I saw it from up above, just before you came upon it."

He waved her behind him and levered the sled on its side for a shield. They stripped off their skis, then hunkered down behind the sled. Jack fashioned a sort of megaphone with his gloved hands and called out. "Routt County AirLife, this is Rampart Mountain Rescue. Can anyone hear me?"

For the first time in nearly three days, the wind had died down. The quality of silence was eerie, amphitheaterlike. Jack repeated his summons. Again there was no response.

"Okay, look. We'll approach in stages. We have to keep the cornice in mind. We can't afford gunfire, but we can't assume Watkins knows that. I'll go first. I want you to follow. Keep low and don't hesitate to hit the ground." He looked at her. Saw what she supposed must look like rank fear in her eyes. "Becky, what is it? Are you going to be okay?"

She shook her head, meaning to nod. What could she say? There was no comfort here, no sense that she could possibly win. No chance for her, not if Watkins had survived this.

The deep silence did little to boost her resolve. She trusted Jack Slade with her life, but he had taken real care to remind her, over and over again, that he'd failed once. Even the thought sickened her, even the way it sprang to her mind when she knew how he loved her and knew absolutely that, no matter what, Jack would watch over her and sacrifice his life in a split second to save hers.

But against the likes of Michael Watkins, would it be enough, or only a terrible waste?

She pulled off a mitten and lay her bare hand on his cheek. She felt trapped in the path of some formless tide of reckoning coming straight at her, a reckoning over which she had no control or defense—even with Jack close at hand.

She tried to shake it. Offering a saucy grin and stroking his jaw. "It's just... I'd rather hurl myself into a volcano to appease the gods than do this, is all."

He would have laughed, because he knew she meant to make light of her fears, but he didn't have a laugh inside him.

She stuffed her hand into her mitten and lowered her voice to a whisper. "Let's just get this over with, okay?"

He took a few seconds to straighten her hood. "You be careful, you hear me?"

"I hear you." *You, too.*

He got to his feet before he could think any more, crouched low, cleared the barrier of the sled and took off for an outcropping of snow-covered granite about a quarter of the way to the crash site. She waited for his signal, then followed more or less in his tracks.

Twice they repeated the process. Each time Jack called out, identifying themselves, asking for anyone alive to respond.

For the first time, a sound, a low groan, maybe, drifted toward them.

Jack perked up his ears. "AirLife! Is that you?"

"Slade?" The voice was weak, thready. "Jack…is that you?"

"Yeah, this is Slade—"

"Jack…" The voice drifted off. "Thank God."

The relief inside her was so intense, so palpable, Becky sank to her knees in the snow. Jack shook his head at her, warning against dropping her guard, but he couldn't disguise his hope that all their fears had been for nothing.

"AirLife, take it easy," he called. "Help is on the way. Tell me who you are, who's on board."

"Jack, it's Kip—" His voice broke. "It's Kip Farris." Jack nodded to Becky, confirming that he knew the name. "Flight nurse—June's—dead. No other survivors."

"You take it easy, Kip," Jack called. "Don't move. We're on our way." He turned to Becky. "I want you to wait here. Just let me confirm what he said."

"Jack, we've got to get him—"

"No. What we've got to do is not be stupid. Another few seconds isn't going to make a difference. You wait."

"All right, just go. Go!"

He began to make his way toward the chopper. "Kip, listen, talk to me, buddy. Can you see daylight? Tell me what you see. Are you pinned in?"

"Jack. You gotta…you gotta help…me. No," he shouted deliriously. "That's not right! You gotta get outta—" The pilot broke off with an excruciating cry of pain.

Jack flinched, spun around and broke into a run toward her. She screamed at him, "Jack, wait! What are you doing! You have to—"

But a shot rang out, zinging past Jack's head, then a second and third, and she knew they had been tricked. He flew at her from three yards out, knocked her to the ground and fell, covering her, but a fourth shot glanced off the wall of granite beside her, and shards like needles pelted her in the face and eyes. She screamed out in pain.

Swearing vilely, Jack dragged her through the snow, shielding her with his body, then drew on some superhuman strength to get her behind a granite outcropping. She couldn't open her right eye, but through her left she saw her blood staining the snow.

Gritting her teeth against the pain and terror, she scooped up a gob of snow and plastered it to the right side of her face. Shedding his rifle holster, Jack shoved up tight against the side of a boulder and pulled her into his lap, cradling her body in his. "Becky, let me see."

"No, Jack! What's happening?" Freezing cold, scared witless, she refused to give up. "Let me go!"

she cried. "Just stop it, Jack! We've got to help him!"

"We will, Becky." He caught her flailing arms and pried her gloved hand away from her face, murmuring constant reassurances until she could relax her arm and let him brush away the snow of her makeshift poultice. "We will, but first you have to let me see your eyes."

Tears eked out both her eyes and she shivered violently. "Jack, how—" Her voice broke. She gritted her teeth. "How bad is it?"

He shook his head. "These are nasty cuts, Becky, but there isn't a speck of stone or dirt."

"Ice shards, then?"

Nodding, he stuck the middle finger of his glove between his teeth and pulled his hand out. He stroked her bloodied cheek. "Can you let me check your eye?"

She shook her head, choking on her tears. "He's there, isn't he? He made Kip say those things to draw us in—"

"Shh, Becky, listen to me. He's there, but we can't do anything until I see what's happened to your eye."

She gave a quick nod, forcing herself to relax, letting him gently draw her eyelid up with his thumb.

He swore softly. "It's bleeding, Becky, but the injury is clear of your pupil."

No chunk of granite digging a deeper hole. The

relief inside him couldn't compete with the wrath in his heart. Bare-handed, he scooped snow and placed it against her bruised and bloodied cheek. "You need to keep this iced. Can you pull your hat down far enough in front to patch your eye?"

She knelt in the snow, pulled the end of her scarf up tightly against and over the snow on the right side of her face, then yanked her ski cap over the scarf. "Jack, what are we going to do? He's there. He's got Kip. God knows what he did to him when he cried out to warn you."

"I'll kill the son of a bitch with my own two hands," Jack swore.

"You'll never get close enough." Battling tears of frustration, she clenched her teeth and shrugged. "Watkins has got nothing to lose, Jack. Nothing at all. There's no way out of this for him," she cried, "and the only thing he has left to do is take us out with him."

"Rampart? Are you still there?" The mocking voice could only be Watkins's. "Rampart?"

Jack pulled his rifle from the leather casing. "Who's asking?"

"Who do you think, Jackie boy? Just who do you suppose you're dealing with?"

Becky clapped the back of her fist over her mouth. The taunt hit her harder, far harder than the wild shot that had driven shards of ice into her face. The snow continued to dump from the skies. The wind had virtually died. Watkins could be no closer that fifty feet, but she heard him as well as she heard Jack.

He shot her a cautioning look. If Watkins understood he had hurt her, their position would be worse.

"There's only one way out of this for you, Watkins. Give up your hostage, and we'll talk."

Watkins laughed. "I've got a deal for you, Jackie boy. You give up your little piece of tail, and then we won't even have to talk."

Jack lowered his head. His jaw ached. He only thought he knew, before this, what it was to feel murder banging around in his heart. "That's not going to happen, Watkins."

"Becky, sweetheart," Watkins taunted, ignoring Jack, "you out there?"

She swallowed hard, looking at Jack for direction. He nodded.

"I'm here."

"I'm touched," Watkins answered. "Daddy's little girl, all grown up. Better tell Jackie boy to back off, sweetheart, and give yourself up, or the chopper jockey here gets the first one-way ticket out of this hellhole."

She bit her lip and swallowed, shaking her head. "Jack, he means it. He'll never back off—"

He held up a hand. "What's the condition of your pilot, Watkins?"

"Are you deaf, Jack?" Watkins bellowed. "D'you think I won't blow this jerk-off pilot away?"

"Do you think you'll have a bargaining position left if you do?"

"Are you really fool enough to try jerking me around, Jack?" Watkins snarled. "You have *one* chance to save a life here. It won't do to piss me off."

"Tell you what, Watkins," Jack snapped angrily. "I've got what you want, and there's no freaking way you're going to give up your only bargaining chip, so—"

"Don't be an ignorant ass, Jack!" Watkins jeered. "Maybe you haven't heard, but there was a nasty little train derailment in Denver when Rabbit Foot Hill went up."

Chapter Twelve

Becky smothered her cry in her mittens. Jack drew his fist over his brow. There was no doubt in either of their minds that, bluffing or not, Watkins held all the cards.

"The explosion must have triggered some kind of chain reaction. If he's not lying, Becky, if it happened, it happened, and there was never anything you could do about it."

She shook her head. Fresh tears clogged her throat. "If I hadn't taken so long to identify him. If—"

"No. He had an ironclad plan, and he sucked you in. It's what he's wanted all along, to make you take on his guilt. To blame yourself."

"Very interesting analysis, Jack. But I'm tired and cold and a little short-tempered, so what do you say we get on with it?"

Stunned that Watkins had heard him, Jack turned

to Becky, gestured to his own ear and mouthed a silent question. *How could he hear us?*

She shrugged. *A directional mike?*

Jack shook his head. *No way.* In a normal voice he asked, "What do you want, Watkins?"

"I was thinking something along the lines of a trade-off." Watkins must be shouting, but he had obviously heard Jack clearly.

"What trade-off?"

"Let me make this simple for you, Jack. You're out of this deal. Becky gets to decide, just like her daddy playing God. You getting this, Becky? Either you give yourself up or the sixteen square city blocks surrounding the Denver Mint get transformed into a crater. What's it going to be, sweetheart? Who lives and who dies?"

Jack had no idea what Watkins meant about her father playing God, but it hardly mattered.

She gritted her teeth. "I'm not my father, Watkins. I don't make those decisions."

She had lowered her voice even more than Jack. Still, Watkins heard her. "Choose, or no one makes it out alive, Becky. Like you said, I've got nothing left to lose."

Jack signaled for her to keep up the dialogue. Discouraged, she shoved another handful of snow beneath her scarf and rested her head.

In his own worst nightmares, he could not have produced a scenario as perverse as this—in the frozen and relentlessly unforgiving mountains, he was cut out of the negotiations, and Becky found herself horse trading with her own life, not even able to see her nemesis.

She held the back of her mittened hand to her face, fighting the pain, scrambling for something to say.

"Make him deal," Jack murmured. "You're doing fine. We have to know whether the mint is set to blow or if he will trigger it from here."

She nodded and dragged in a shaky breath. "I need to know that you won't kill Kip anyway, Watkins. I need some guarantee that the mint isn't already set to blow on a timer."

"You're not exactly in a position to be asking for guarantees, Becky," Watkins warned her nastily. "Are you questioning my integrity?"

She choked on a wild bubble of laughter in her throat. "It's only a bad habit of mine, Watkins," she snapped.

Jack put a hand on her arm. *Easy.* "The bomb, Becky," he whispered.

"Jack, he's not going to tell me that!" she cried softly. "He wouldn't have left it to chance, and he won't settle!"

As desperate in his heart as she, Jack reached out to her, cupping the back of her neck, cradling her head next to his. "If you believe that, Becky," he whispered into her ear, "then cut the deal. Tell him you need a few minutes, half an hour. Tell him to send Kip out, and you'll turn yourself over to him.''

She began to shake hard, deep, silent sobs racking her body.

''Becky, love, stop. Listen to me.'' He swallowed, looked to where he knew the cornice hung so precariously. ''I'll make my way up the mountain as far as I can get so I can trigger an avalanche.''

She pulled back, her dark, glittering eyes wide. He thought she saw the possibilities. ''You walk out as if you're going to meet Kip in the middle,'' he went on in muffled tones, ''and then keep on going. You won't be within range of Watkins's gun till you pass the midpoint, but you're never going to do that. The minute Kip's close enough to see what you're doing, you turn and run like hell. Both of you. Can you do that, Becky, while I set off the avalanche?''

''Yes.'' She nodded. The possibility of a way out had energized her.

''Okay.'' He turned from her and made an insolent remark about Watkins and the absence of any kind of integrity to provoke him.

''Stay the hell out of it, Slade,'' Watkins returned. ''If I want your opinion, I'll let you know. I'm dealing with Becky now. You keep your mouth shut until and unless I ask you to say one good goddamn word!''

Jack clinched his fist. Watkins had taken the bait.

If he didn't hear from Jack, his suspicions would not be aroused.

"Listen." He took Becky by the shoulders. "I may not be able to control the direction, but if you can get below that outcropping of boulders, the snowslide won't take you down."

She battled her tears furiously. "And if we're very, very lucky, it *will* bury Watkins alive."

He'd become a believer in the power of her wishes. He knew she would wish very, very hard for that outcome. What he didn't know was how he could tolerate leaving her. He cupped her face in his hand, touched his brow to hers, his nose to hers in the briefest Eskimo kiss...his lips to hers in a real kiss, less brief, more immodest, full of promise, bereft of any wish ever to leave her.

She pushed him away. "You come back to me, Jack," she murmured.

"I'll be back, Becky. I'll be back," he whispered.

He'd never been much of a believer in the power of his own wishes, but all he could think of, climbing toward the cornice, was the possibility of getting his careless wish to have lived hard and died young.

BECKY STEELED HERSELF to keep Watkins dangling. She needed time for Jack to get up the mountainside far enough to set off an avalanche without being consumed by it. She played out the scenario he had described. Watkins went along with her plan.

She should have known.

"It's time, little girl. Time to show your face. Be a clever girl now and tell Jack goodbye."

Panic roiled through her. She forced herself to get out the words Watkins expected. "Goodbye, Jack."

"That's a girl. *Now,* Jack. Now we'll hear from you. Tell Becky goodbye."

Her heart seemed to stop, her mind to go blank. There was nothing she could do. Nothing.

"Jack?" Watkins called testily. "I can't hear you, Jack."

She sprang up and left the protection of the granite outcropping. "Leave it alone, Watkins. This is between you and me," she cried. "If I'm going to die, the least you can do is look me in the face!"

"Oh, my, my, my! I'll bet Jackie boy's gone off to play hero, hasn't he? Well, then, there really is nothing left but for us to meet."

"Fine. I'm coming now." She yanked up the snow gaiter protecting her pant leg and boot from the deep snow and took out her gun, then replaced the gaiter. She tightened her scarf and stood ready to make her way through the drifts of snow Jack had broken up.

She wanted desperately to look up the mountainside, to find Jack. The snowfall had finally begun to abate. There was a possibility she could spot him. She needed a glimpse of him, one last glimpse. She needed it more than her next breath of air. But Watkins would be watching her, and she would only give Jack's position away.

She grew impatient waiting for Watkins to show himself. Tears threatened to blur the vision in her good eye. Resentment churned inside her. She felt like a puppet on a wire, a marionette without a will of her own, a wooden dummy tossed carelessly into the wrong hands, the wrong act.

Most of all she felt cheated and outraged.

She might go down, but she would not go easy. She seized upon one possibility. The strange acoustics of the atmosphere had allowed Watkins to hear even their lowest voices. If luck were just this once on her side, Jack would hear her. All she had to do was find a way to let him know that if anyone came walking toward her, it must be Watkins himself because it could not be Kip Farris.

"I think I've changed my mind, Watkins," she called loudly, making her way toward him. *Ready, Jack. Please be ready for anything,* she thought. "If I don't get to see Kip, if I'm going to die, the least you can do is spare me ever having to look at you. Just take your shot now and spare me."

"Spare me." There came a sound that confounded her, a barking, flat laugh she had heard somewhere. A figure emerged from behind the massive lump of twisted wreckage, wraithlike through the fog of a grounded cloud, dressed in heavy storm clothes so she might never recognize him.

''Take your shot now and spare me,'' the figure said.

''Gunnar?'' Her head began to throb. Her throat refused to work. ''Gunnar?'' she cried. Dear God. ''Gunnar, what are you doing? Where is Watkins?''

''Where is Watkins?'' he repeated dumbly, without expression, shaking his head. ''Gunnar only knows Hennessy.''

It had to be Gunnar. She couldn't see his face because of the hood he wore, but it *was* Gunnar. He spoke of himself in the third person, and in Gunnar's flat, monotonous tone. But some stray detail, some inconsequential aspect was dreadfully wrong. Something...his clothes.

His coat.

The three-cornered tear with the stuffing spilling out. The coat belonged to the man Gunnar knew only as Mick Hennessy.

Yep. That's old Mick. See here. Had that tear in his coat too long. Too long, Gunnar told him. Better fix it 'efore all the stuffin's gone out.

She stopped dead in her tracks, dead in her heart, cold dread gripping her. Mick Hennessy was Michael Watkins—and so was Gunnar Schmit, and she was to be the one to pay the piper.

Disbelief washed over her.

Horror.

Gunnar Schmit knew Jack's FBI reputation not because he had spilled his guts in some drunken stupor, but because Michael Watkins knew the Denver bureau.

Gunnar really hadn't given a damn if they ever made it to the crash site. He was never worried, never in the least concerned that his "friend" Mick Hennessy might have been injured in the crash or was suffering exposure—because whoever it was that had been evacuated from Rabbit Foot Hill, it wasn't Michael Watkins.

Gunnar Schmit was Michael Watkins, and Gunnar Schmit was busy amusing himself playing cat-and-mouse games with her in a match she had never, till now, understood.

Everything came sickeningly clear at last, every unexplained detail, the reasons, the way he knew her father was a drunk—everything except why Watkins was doing this at all.

He stood only ten or twelve feet from her, a slow, maniacal smile spreading over his face. "Poor Becky. Such a shock it must be. What happened to your face?"

"I'm a little bloodied." She gritted her teeth. If he thought she would be willing to play the prey in his sick cat-and-mouse games any longer, he had another thought coming. She would show him no fear. She had none to show. "But I am far from defeated, Watkins."

"Far from defeated," he mocked in Gunnar's voice, then sneered. "I see you brought your gun.

Why don't you just use it? I know why I haven't used mine quite yet, but I'm trying to understand why you haven't used yours. Hmm... There must be a very good reason.''

"There is.'' She couldn't use it, not without risking a premature triggering of the avalanche and Jack's life with it, but she gave Watkins another reason. "I want to know what it is you want, Watkins. Why the games? What's the point?''

He shook his head. "You know what? I didn't even know myself. Not that I didn't have every intention of making a statement, and making it clearly to your father—''

"Wasn't murdering my mother enough?'' she cried.

"No,'' he answered patiently, as if she were some dullard child he had to lead by the hand through the complexities of a game of Chutes and Ladders. "It wasn't. It turned out not to be. I thought to make him pay one more time, with your life, but it all became so much more intriguing when you and Jack showed up so desperately in love. Then, you see, Gunnar knew—I knew—that one of you could truly be made to understand. One of you would live, the other die.''

Her horror mounted. "What have you done with Kip?''

"His legs were already broken. He shouldn't have

tried to warn Jack off, though. Since then, he's been unconscious.''

She began to shake. "And Rosenberg? What happened to Sam?''

Watkins's eyes narrowed. His face, Gunnar's gentle, simple face hardened. "Rosenberg is the corpse. You shouldn't have sent him.''

Her shaking had more to do with rage than cold, though she had never been more chilled through to her bones. "How high does the body count have to get before you will be finally satisfied?''

Watkins shrugged. "Rosenberg got in the way. Complicated things. I must say, you've led a merry chase. But now, I'm afraid I'm going to have to ask you to put down your gun.''

She tossed her weapon at his feet. "I'm unarmed now. Will you shoot an unarmed woman?'' She made the taunt to signal Jack. "Or should I turn and walk away from you so you can shoot me in the back? Who will ever know, after all, who shot who?''

He grew instantly suspicious and raised his gun, pointing it directly at her face. "Where's Jack?'' he snarled.

"Watkins!''

For his answer, from above, Jack fired his high-powered rifle to disable Watkins. Watkins's gun went flying, and he bellowed in pain. Becky ducked as Jack had instructed her to do, but the avalanche that resulted took Jack down with it.

DESPITE THE MOST intensive search-and-rescue mission launched since the military jet carrying live atomic weapons had gone down near Aspen the year before, Jack's body had not been recovered.

She felt more frozen, more numb inside than she would have been if she had been the one caught in the massive snowslide. She stood staring through the two-way mirror outside an interrogation room in the Denver offices of the Colorado Bureau of Investigation.

Michael Watkins sat chained to the table, his hands cuffed in front of him to accommodate the shoulder wound Jack had managed to inflict. Aguilar stood beside her.

"You don't have to do this, Becky."

"I know." She understood that, in principle, she did not have to deal with Watkins. Joe would go to the mat for her over it, but in truth she had very little choice.

Watkins had refused an attorney. He intended to plead guilty to all and sundry charges. His only condition for saving the Colorado taxpayers the millions of dollars it would take to prosecute him was that his statement be taken by Becky Difalco.

He didn't care how many people were present. All he wanted was to sit across from her.

The state's attorneys numbered five. The gallery was already assembled and in place. Watkins rarely so much as blinked, but the smirk on his face had a mind-numbing quality. For herself, already half-numbed to extinction, Becky had no fear.

She straightened, pulling down on her jacket. "Let's get this over with." She let herself into the room and took the chair opposite Watkins. The video cam behind her began to roll.

Watkins's smirk faded. His expression went blank, and he became Gunnar Schmit. The cunning, the complete transition of evil incarnate to harmlessness, the brilliance behind the village idiot facade was intended, she thought, to unnerve her. She chose, instead, to label her reaction fascination.

She went through the preliminaries for the record, identifying herself, the location, date and time. "State your name, age, occupation and address for the record, please."

His eyes bored into her. "Michael Aaron Watkins, age fifty-three, resident of Rampart, Colorado, PO Box 34, part-time bartender, occasional domestic...terrorist." He leaned in. "Are you lonesome at night yet, Becky?"

"Would that make you happy, Mick?"

"Happy?" He shrugged. "I forgot what happy feels like a ways back." His face darkened. "Twenty-five *years* back. It would, however, give me a cheap thrill."

Surprised to have provoked the smallest reaction from him, she sat back, crossing one black-stockinged leg over the other. "You'll understand if providing your cheap thrills doesn't interest me, Gunnar."

"Mick."

"Mick, then. Let's start at the beginning, say 1969?"

"An auspicious year." He rattled off arcane social and political details leading up to and surrounding the years in which he had conducted one act of terrorism after another. The burgeoning drug culture, the assassination of Bobby Kennedy, the Vietnam War, the paranoia of the times.

The riots at the Democratic National Convention in Chicago in 1968 set him on his course. Championing the cause of redistributing the nation's wealth, he had killed nearly two hundred people. Martyrs, he called them. Victims—not his, but of cultural greed.

If pressed, he could name them, each and every one.

Becky refused the offer. She didn't want to hear her mother's name come out of his vile mouth, or the names of all the other innocents. She found his story chilling beyond her own dire expectations, beyond any physical chill she had experienced in the long, terrifying night before her rescue. Coming from the mouth of a man she had believed absolutely incapable of putting together three sentences of his own, his account was not only lucid. She found it, on some despicably, dazzlingly twisted level, quite compelling.

His confessions took nearly two hours. The videographer interrupted to reload the cameras. Watkins sat back, regarding her closely.

At the videographer's signal, she began again. "Tell me about Gunnar."

"Tell me about Gunnar," he mocked in Gunnar's simpleton voice, then reverted to his own voice. "Gunnar was a very comfortable role for me to play. I'm not sure your daddy would even have recognized me." He looked directly into the videocam. "How about it, Louis?"

Becky swallowed. "My father isn't here."

"Of course not," Watkins said, sneering. "Why should he be? But the point is, no one really looks at the village idiot, you see. With such a creature is not where one expects to find a terrorist lurking." He gave a laugh. "Gunnar even fooled our man Jack, didn't he? Who was more likely than Jack to be acquainted with the mug shots on the most wanted lists?

"It amused me endlessly," he went on. "I learned things one simply cannot imagine. For instance…" Watkins focused on her eyes. "Did you know that you had quite ruined Jack for other women?"

Her heart stilled. Joe Aguilar wasn't the only one who had warned her Watkins would at some point go for her emotional jugular. The bevy of attorneys at her back had the huge majority of what they wanted. All she had to do was get up and leave to end the interview, but she still had questions—important questions.

"I don't believe you."

He shrugged his good shoulder. "I don't care if you do." He had no reason to lie to her, not after confessing to the most heinous crimes of the century. No reason but to provoke her. "But it's quite true," he assured her evenly. "In all the years Jack spent in Rampart, the poor jerk never managed to get it up. It wasn't for lack of opportunity, either."

"You are truly a slug and a bastard, Watkins." She stared at him. Heat and confusion suffused her body, and her throat convulsed. She both believed and despised him. "How dare you?"

"How dare I." His head swiveled on his neck like a sprung jack-in-the-box. "How dare I. Let me see…" He laughed. The chains at his wrists rattled. "How do you manage to sit here and listen for three hours to the grisly details of my career and then wonder how I dare spill Jack's guts? And on the record, no less, for all to see and hear? Tell me," he urged. "Maybe you can still rehabilitate Jack's reputation—for the record. Did he manage, before he died, to get it up one last time?"

"You can quite imagine it, can't you?" she retorted. "Why is that, Mick, or would you prefer Gunnar in this context?"

"You bore me." He managed to turn his chair to the side, and she was gratified to notice a slight wince of pain at the jarring of his shoulder. "I'm tired of you. Run along now, little girl, before you burn your fingers."

"It's you. You're the one who never managed to make love to a woman after Maeve, isn't that it?"

"We were discussing Jack, and I assure you, the tale is his...so to speak."

"No." She shook her head. "It's you."

"I won't warn you again, little girl."

She refused to heed him. What had he left to hurt her with? She sat back. "What a relief it must have been to slip into being Gunnar. To hide in the guise of the village idiot, certain, at least, that no woman would ever get close enough to know."

"Astute." He commended her, nodding. "Very, very...astute."

By any standards, Michael Watkins deserved the pain he'd inflicted on the lives of more innocent people than she dared imagine, but in his terribly neutral tone, she heard in him the volume, the sheering emotion, the cracking open of pain along decades-old fault lines.

"As yet, of course," he went on, seemingly idly, "you have only a whiff of any real comprehension of the pain involved in losing Jack. But you are a clever girl. Definitely on the learning curve.'' He shook his head, eyeing her with a terrible empathy. ''Poor Becky. You never answered my question, sweetheart. Have you begun to miss him yet?''

''I don't know.'' She stared at her hands, wondering if what she felt could be labeled missing Jack. ''Do you still miss Maeve?''

''No.''

''You're a liar,'' she accused.

''No.''

But she saw in his pitiless stare a flicker of heated emotion. ''No?''

''No.'' He sniffed in disdain. ''Check back with me in twenty-five years. See if *you* can remember. See if *you* miss what you can't freaking remember, *Becky.*''

She lifted her chin. ''I'll remember.''

''Really?'' His brows lifted. ''You'll remember? How extraordinary! Do you think you will recall what his skin smelled like? Do you think you'll actually remember what he tasted of? How Jack breathed, how Jack ate, how Jack slept? How he touched you? Tell me.'' Like an owl fixing on its prey in the dead of night, Watkins stretched his neck. ''How did he touch you, Becky?''

Tears pricked her eyelids. Swearing, Joe Aguilar jerked the door open to end the interview, but she held up a hand to prevent his interruption.

She understood, finally, what had driven him. The loss of Maeve felt the same to him as what she felt over the loss of Jack, and there would always be a part of her that could never condemn what Watkins had done to her, because what had been done to him was as dreadful as anything, anything she knew.

He was still lashing out in his pain and his anger. "Do you remember how it felt when he made love to you? Can you remember even now? Can you? *Can you? Damn it, woman, answer me!* Can you remember, even now, the sound of his voice?"

"She won't need to remember it, Watkins. Not for a very long time."

Her eyes flew to the door, where she had believed only Aguilar stood waiting to help her, and there, with his arm in a cast and his eyebrow slit and stitched and scabbed over, stood Jack.

When he smiled, she cried. She had no idea how he had survived, but with Jack, the how rarely mattered. His promises were as good as her wishes, and she had, finally, someone to watch over her, and someone to watch over in return.

DEBBIE MACOMBER

invites you to the

★ ♥ ★ HEART OF TEXAS ★ ★

Join Debbie Macomber as she brings you the lives
and loves of the folks in the ranching community
of Promise, Texas.

If you loved Midnight Sons—don't miss
Heart of Texas! A brand-new six-book series
from Debbie Macomber.

Available in February 1998
at your favorite retail store.

Heart of Texas by Debbie Macomber

Lonesome Cowboy	February '98
Texas Two-Step	March '98
Caroline's Child	April '98
Dr. Texas	May '98
Nell's Cowboy	June '98
Lone Star Baby	July '98

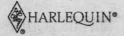

KEY TO MY HEART

Unlock the secrets of romance just in time for the most romantic day of the year— Valentine's Day!

Key to My Heart
features three of your favorite authors,

Kasey Michaels,
Rebecca York
and Muriel Jensen,

to bring you wonderful tales of romance and Valentine's Day dreams come true.

As an added bonus you can receive Harlequin's special Valentine's Day necklace. FREE with the purchase of every *Key to My Heart* collection.

Available in January,
wherever Harlequin books are sold.

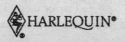

HARLEQUIN®

PHKEY349

ATTENTION:
FANS OF 43 LIGHT STREET!

Join us next month for a very special "43 Light Street" tale, when Rebecca York takes her best-loved series to a masked Valentine's Day ball. Don't miss "Remington and Juliet"—Rebecca York's debut short story in the romantic Valentine's Day short story collection

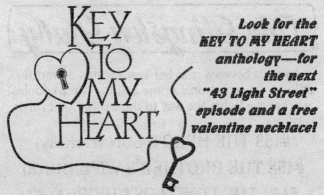

Look for the
KEY TO MY HEART
anthology—for
the next
"43 Light Street"
episode and a free
valentine necklace!

Don't miss KEY TO MY HEART—available in February, wherever Harlequin books are sold.

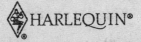

HARLEQUIN®
INTRIGUE®

In the mountains of Colorado, the snow comes in on a gust of wind, reaching blizzard conditions in a matter of minutes. Here, the Rampart Mountain Rescue Team is never lonely. But this year there's even more activity than usual for the team, as not only Mother Nature but mystery is swirling in their midst.

Rocky Mtn. RESCUE

Join three of your favorite Intrigue authors for an intimate look at the lives and loves of the men and women of one of America's highest mountain rescue teams. It's the place to be for thrills, chills and adventure!

Don't miss

**#449 FORGET ME NOT by Cassie Miles
January 1998**

**#454 WATCH OVER ME by Carly Bishop
February 1998**

**#459 FOLLOW ME HOME by Leona Karr
March 1998**

**Look for these titles—
available at your favorite retail outlet!**

January 1998
Renegade Son by Lisa Jackson

Danielle Summers had problems: a rebellious child
and unscrupulous enemies. In addition, her Montana
ranch was slowly being sabotaged. And then there was
Chase McEnroe—who admired her land and desired her
body. But Danielle feared he would invade more than just
her property—he'd trespass on her heart.

February 1998
The Heart's Yearning by Ginna Gray

Fourteen years ago Laura gave her baby up for adoption,
and not one day had passed that she didn't think about
him and agonize over her choice—so she finally followed
her heart to Texas to see her child. But the plan to watch
her son from afar doesn't quite happen that way, once the
boy's sexy—*single*—father takes a decided interest in *her*.

March 1998
First Things Last by Dixie Browning

One look into Chandler Harrington's dark eyes and
Belinda Massey could refuse the Virginia millionaire nothing.
So how could the no-nonsense nanny believe the rumors that
he had kidnapped his nephew—an adorable, healthy little boy
who crawled as easily into her heart as he did into her lap?

**BORN IN THE USA: Love, marriage—
and the pursuit of family!**

 HARLEQUIN® ▼ *Silhouette*®

Look us up on-line at: http://www.romance.net

BUSA4

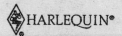 **HARLEQUIN®**

Not The Same Old Story!

 **HARLEQUIN PRESENTS®**

Exciting, glamorous romance stories that take readers around the world.

Harlequin Romance®

Sparkling, fresh and tender love stories that bring you pure romance.

HARLEQUIN™ Temptation.

Bold and adventurous— Temptation is strong women, bad boys, great sex!

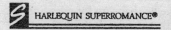 **HARLEQUIN SUPERROMANCE®**

Provocative and realistic stories that celebrate life and love.

 **HARLEQUIN® AMERICAN ROMANCE®**

Contemporary fairy tales—where anything is possible and where dreams come true.

HARLEQUIN® INTRIGUE®

Heart-stopping, suspenseful adventures that combine the best of romance and mystery.

 **LOVE & LAUGHTER™**

Humorous and romantic stories that capture the lighter side of love.

Look us up on-line at: http://www.romance.net   HGENERIC